ROCK MY WORLD

Cindi Myers

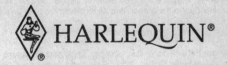

HARLEQUIN®

TORONTO • NEW YORK • LONDON
AMSTERDAM • PARIS • SYDNEY • HAMBURG
STOCKHOLM • ATHENS • TOKYO • MILAN • MADRID
PRAGUE • WARSAW • BUDAPEST • AUCKLAND

Thanks to John Craft for answering my questions about radio. Any mistakes in this manuscript are my fault, not John's.

ISBN 0-373-79219-0

ROCK MY WORLD

1

"I TELL YOU, NICK, this is gonna be great. The whole city will be talking about this one."

Erica Gibson froze outside the office of the station manager of radio station KROK, her arms full of demo CDs, press packets, contest entries and miscellaneous envelopes that had arrived in the day's mail. Six months of working as an intern/assistant/general flunky at the station had taught her that these were dangerous words. Station manager Carl Husack was forever hatching wild schemes to promote KROK (pronounced *kay-rock*, not *crock* he had warned her, her first day on the job. This despite the cartoon drawing of a dancing crocodile that appeared in almost every advertisement for the station.) Staff didn't want to get too close to Carl when he was in full gonzo promo mood or they'd find themselves dressed like chickens passing out flyers in the parking lot at a Broncos game or hurtling down a ski slope wearing nothing but flesh-colored bikinis and strategically placed KROK stickers—both stunts to which previous interns had been subjected.

"Tell me again, because I can't believe I heard you right." Morning show host "Naughty" Nick Cassidy sprawled on the leather sofa across from Carl's desk.

Erica could just make out the silver-tipped toes of his black alligator boots.

"A bed-in," Carl said. "You broadcast for seventy-five hours from a king-size bed in the main showroom of Mattress Max's Furniture Gallery."

Erica made a face. Mattress Max was the station's biggest advertiser, known for his in-your-face, used-car-salesman approach to selling furniture. "You can't beat a Mattress Max deal!" he screamed in commercials that aired on KROK twenty times a day.

"A bed-in." Nick's trademark sultry drawl tended to sound more like a croaking frog when he wasn't "on." "What's so fascinating about me sitting in bed cuing up CDs?"

"You don't just cue up CDs. We'll make it a fund-raiser. People come by and donate money for the new homeless shelter the Salvation Army is building in Aurora. Get it—a bed-in to raise money for more beds for the homeless?"

The more Carl talked, the more he sounded like Mattress Max, with that same frantic quality.

"I don't know, Carl. It sounds boring as hell."

"Not boring. Not boring at all. It wouldn't just be you in the bed. We'd put one of the female jocks with you. The public will love it."

Nick leaned forward. Now Erica could see the wave of ink-black hair that dipped over his forehead, and the end of his nose jutting out like the prow of a ship. He had, as Carl himself said, "A face only radio could love," but that didn't stop him from making time with every female who crossed his path. In fact, the whole Naughty Nick show was based on the premise that he was the biggest player in Denver. And as of last month, it was the top-rated morning drive-time show among the coveted demographic of twenty-four to fifty-four-year-olds.

"Now I'm getting interested," Nick said. "Who's the lucky lady?"

"I don't know yet. It's not like we've got a lot to choose from. There's Audra Benson, the late-night gal."

"She's seven months pregnant!"

Erica stifled a laugh at the horror in Nick's voice.

"What about Bombshell Bonnie? She's hot."

"Bombshell" Bonnie Remington was the station's weather and traffic "girl," a bleached blonde whose main claim to fame was once having posed for a *Playboy* feature on "Wild Women of Rock Radio" and her short-lived affair with afternoon drive-time jock Adam "the Hawk" Hawkins. Right before Erica came on staff Bonnie and Adam had apparently had a very public bust-up and in the months since the chill between them could have air-conditioned the building.

"Bonnie'll never do it," Nick said.

"Why not? She's always whining about wanting more airtime. And she's already proved she's an exhibitionist."

"Let me put it another way—I won't do it with Bonnie."

"Why not? She's a knockout. The two of you will go over great together."

"No way. The woman's a ball breaker. You heard how she raked the Hawk over the coals when they called it quits."

"We won't have any more problems like that. You know the rules."

"If you think forbidding dating among the on-air staff is going to solve all your problems, you don't know Bonnie. I tried flirting with her once and she ripped me a new one before the commercial break was over. I don't want anything to do with her."

"Then who? It ain't like we've got two dozen females hanging around the station who aren't going to freeze up in front of a microphone."

"What about that intern—Erline or whatever her name is?"

"Erica? You mean Erica, who managed to piss off not one, but *two* advertising accounts *and* draw an FCC fine the one and only time I let her near a microphone?"

Nick laughed, and Erica stifled a groan. Was it her fault she'd been shoved on the air at the last minute to fill in for Audra, who was in the ladies' room, puking up her dinner? Anyone could have mixed up the commercials. And she hadn't realized her microphone was still live when she started cursing her inability to straighten things out. She'd had to beg Carl not to fire her, and since then, he hadn't let her near the broadcast booth.

Nick's laughter finally subsided. "Come on, Carl. It's not like she screwed up on purpose. And she'll have me there to show her the ropes."

"Just make sure that's all you show her," Carl said. "I suppose it wouldn't hurt to give her a try…."

Did that mean Carl was going to let her do this? A live promo? She hardly had time to absorb the idea before the stack of mail shifted and began sliding. As CDs and Tyvek mailers tumbled to the floor, she let loose a stream of words that definitely were not allowed on air.

"Who's making all that racket? We're trying to have a meeting in here." Carl stuck his head out the door. "Oh, Erica, it's you. Come in here a minute." Not waiting for an answer, he took her arm and hustled her into the office.

Nick looked her up and down and offered one of his trademark smarmy smiles. "Hello, beautiful."

Nick called every woman "beautiful," even if she was dressed like a bag lady and wearing a fright wig. "Hey, Nick." She turned to Carl, trying to look innocent. "What's up?"

Carl leaned against the desk. He was a short man with a wide face and jug-handle ears, dressed in green cords and a striped button-down shirt and red Chuck Taylors. He reminded Erica of a garden gnome. "How long have you been working here, Erica?" he asked.

"Six months." As he very well knew.

"I think it's about time we gave you some more airtime, don't you?"

She cut her eyes over to Nick, who was grinning at her as though she was the special of the day. As if his player act impressed her. She focused again on Carl. "That *is* the reason I took this job." It was bad enough a few detours in her career path made her one of the oldest interns in the history of the station—she didn't plan to spend any longer than she had to shlepping mail and fetching coffee. She had her sights set on an on-air slot at the top rock station in Denver.

"Great!" Carl clapped his hands together. "We've got a fantastic new promo coming up that'll pair you on air with Nick for three days next month. Not just the morning show, but live spots during the day as well. Terrific exposure."

She glanced at Nick again, who leered at her. Three days in bed with *that*. She shuddered. "What exactly *is* the promo?" How would Carl spin this one?

"A fund-raiser for the new homeless shelter. Great, huh? Mattress Max came to me with the idea and I knew we had to get on board. Such a great cause." He wasn't looking directly at her anymore, a sure sign he was up to something shady.

"What *exactly* would I have to do?" she asked.

"Oh, nothing difficult. Just broadcast from the show-room floor of Max's Furniture Gallery with Nick here."

"You'd better level with her, Carl." Nick stood, his six-foot-three, thick-set frame towering over her. "You're gonna be spending three days in bed—with me, darlin'."

She glared at the two men, trying to come up with a suitably scathing—yet not job-endangering—answer.

"She's overcome with joy!" Nick patted her back. "Don't worry, darlin'. Naughty Nick will take care of you."

She curled her lip in a close approximation of a snarl. He actually took a step back. It was enough for her to find her voice again. "A bed-in?" She turned to Carl again. "Isn't that a little sleazy?" She thought it was a lot sleazy, but this was, after all, rock radio.

"It's perfectly respectable." Carl put his arm around her. "Think of the great exposure. Think of the home-less shelter. Think how long it'll be before you get an-other chance like this if you turn this one down." His smile faded, along with the gnomelike jolliness. Now he looked like the hard-nosed businessman who had made KROK number one.

She glanced at Nick again. He was still leering. But could any man who ran his mouth that much be serious when it came to action? Besides, she was a grown woman. She could protect herself. And three days on the air! This could make her career. If she passed this up she might as well turn in her resignation and look for another job right now. She turned back to Carl. "All right. But I want a bonus for those three days."

"A bonus!" Carl shook his head. "No can do."

She folded her arms across her chest. "If I'm going to be on-air talent, I deserve a bonus."

"She's got a point there." Nick's hand was heavy on her shoulder. Since he was taking her side, she made herself stand still and not shake him off.

Carl frowned at them for a moment and shook his head. "All right. I'll pay you the same thing an entry-level DJ makes. But just for those three days."

She grinned. "Then we've got a deal."

Carl dropped into his chair. "Great. See Belinda in marketing about getting your picture for the ads. And find something suitable to wear."

Her smile faded. "Suitable?"

"It's a bed-in. People are going to be stopping by, donating money. The two of you need to wear what you'd wear to bed."

Nick chuckled. "In my case, that would be nothing."

She glared at him. His smile vanished. "But I guess since this is for the public, I'll find something a little less revealing. Don't want to shock the folks."

"You don't want to get arrested," Carl said. He turned to Erica. "Sex sells, so let's see some kind of silky lingerie or something. Remember, it's for a good cause."

Right. For a good cause. Her career was a good cause, wasn't it?

She backed out of the office, all chance of a graceful exit ruined when she stumbled over the pile of mail in the doorway. She gathered up the mess of envelopes and mailers and headed down the hall, dizzy from the thoughts racing through her head. Was she crazy? She'd just agreed to spend three days in bed with a man who thought he was a rock and roll Romeo—and she was expected to do it while wearing lingerie? She was out of her mind.

She took the stairs two at a time, racing toward her basement cubicle. Too late, she heard someone coming toward her and looked up in time to collide with a tall, very solid man.

Strong arms steadied her, and her cheek pressed against a broad chest which smelled of starch and Irish Spring. Who would have thought that could be such a sexy combination? She smiled, tempted to plead a sudden weakness and thus stay in his embrace a little longer.

Instead she sighed and pushed out of his arms. "Hey, Adam," she said, brushing her hair out of her eyes. "I'm sorry. I was in a hurry and didn't see you."

"That's okay." Adam Hawkins's brown eyes held an expression of concern. "Everything okay?"

She smiled, trying not to look as flustered as she felt. The truth was, within days of her arrival at the station she'd developed a serious crush on the afternoon jock. Not that he'd paid much attention to her. He was polite, of course, and had at least bothered to learn her name, unlike Nick and some of the others, who expected her to respond to "Hey, you."

But Adam mostly kept to himself around the station. On air he was friendly and warm, but once he took off the microphone, he was a quiet man.

Was there anything sexier than the strong, silent type? Especially when the type in question had broad shoulders, fudge-brown eyes fringed with soot-black lashes, and a bass voice that vibrated right through her whenever he spoke.

Looking at and listening to Adam for hours every day for the past six months, Erica was certain the man had emotional depths and sexual skills just waiting for the right woman—meaning her—to discover.

Too bad their "relationship" so far consisted of mundane comments exchanged in the hall and a few long moments of eye contact.

One more reason to suffer through this gig with Nick. If she did a good job, maybe Adam would start to see her as more than a co-worker. Maybe he'd even wish *he* were in Nick's place in that bed.

Of course, there was still Carl's rule about on-air talent not dating, but she wasn't official on-air talent yet, was she? It was a small loophole, but she wouldn't mind exploiting it with Adam.

"You sure you're okay?" He peered into her face. "You look a little pale."

She nodded, and shifted the stack of mail in her arms. "I'll be fine…eventually."

"What's that supposed to mean? What happened?"

She studied him through lowered lashes, debating

how to break the news. Should she go for sympathy or triumph? "Carl's giving me a new promo gig."

"Oh?" Little worry lines creased his forehead. "What is it this time?"

"It's nothing that bad. It's good, really. Three days of on-air time, raising money for the Salvation Army."

The tension went out of his face. "Three days on air? Hey, that's great."

"Yeah, the only drawback is I'll be working with Nick. Not that he's not a great DJ," she hastened to add. "It's just…"

"It's just that he's Nick." He frowned. "Want me to talk to Carl? See if he can find somebody else?"

The thought that he cared enough to stick up for her made her go weak in the knees. She put her hand on his arm, as much to steady herself as for the chance to touch him. "That's really sweet of you, but I'm okay with it, really. It's a big chance for me."

"Three days is a lot. What's the angle? Some kind of contest or something?"

"Not exactly." Why did she suddenly feel embarrassed? After all, he—and the rest of the city—were going to find out soon enough. "It's a fund-raiser for the new homeless shelter."

"Uh-huh." He looked wary. "So what are you doing to raise the money?"

"We're broadcasting from the showroom of Mattress Max's Furniture Gallery." She took a deep breath, her cheeks hot. "From a…um, a bed."

"A bed?" The frown lines returned, even deeper this time. "You and Naughty Nick in bed for three days?"

She nodded. "It ought to be a blast, don't you think?"

He looked at her a long minute, so long she began to feel a very different heat, this one starting somewhere in her chest and spreading downward, reminding her of some rather explicit sexual fantasies she'd indulged in starring the man in front of her.

But before she could wrap her mind around this idea, his expression relaxed and he patted her shoulder. A friendly, brotherly sort of pat. Not the pat of a man who liked the idea of getting her in bed himself.

"It'll be all right," he said. "I'll talk to Nick myself and make sure he understands that he's to behave like a gentleman."

She would have laughed, except that she was still fighting an attack of lust. *Gentleman* and *Naughty Nick* weren't words that went together. "Thanks. I think I can handle Nick." If nothing else, a firm "no" and a strategically placed shove ought to do the trick. Still, she didn't want Adam to think she didn't need him at all. "Maybe you can stop by the Furniture Gallery and say hello," she said.

"Yeah, uh, maybe I'll do that," he said. He opened his mouth as if to say something else, then shook his head. "I'd better get to work. Good to see you."

"Yeah. Good to see you." She turned and watched him climb the stairs. It was a guilty pleasure she indulged in whenever possible. Word had it a group of female radio personalities had voted it the best ass in radio.

When he was gone, she sighed and headed down the stairs. So much for fantasy. She had to deal with the real world now. She wondered what Carl would say if she showed up at the Furniture Gallery wearing a granny gown and wool socks? That was her preferred winter sleepwear, but she was pretty sure it wasn't what he had in mind.

ADAM HAD EVERY intention of taking a laid-back approach with Carl, making a joke of the whole bed-in project and somehow persuading him to rethink the idea of having Erica participate. He was glad Carl was giving her another chance at on-air time, but in bed—with Nick? Adam's head hurt just thinking about it.

Since the fiasco with Bonnie, he'd made a point of staying away from office politics. But Erica was too nice to turn loose with a player like Nick.

By the time Adam reached the station manager's office he had the makings of a migraine and the first words out of his mouth were "Are you out of your mind?"

Carl looked up from a stack of computer printouts. "Some people would say I'm always out of my mind. Are you referring to anything in particular?"

"This whole bed-in promo with Nick and Erica. It's crazy."

"I agree. It's so crazy it's brilliant. The listeners will love it."

"You don't think it's going a little too far?"

"Hey, it's for charity. And they'll both have clothes on. It's not like they'll be having sex on the air or anything. They'll be doing the regular show, plus live feeds throughout the day. Only they'll be doing them from a bed."

At the mention of Erica and sex in the same sentence he had to sit down. Not that he hadn't thought of her in that context before. More than once he'd caught him-

self admiring her great legs and indulging in fantasies
of them wrapped around him. Women like her—petite,
blond and curvy—were definitely his weakness, one he
tried to keep under control. It helped to remind himself
she was just a kid. She didn't look a day over seventeen, though he figured she was at least twenty-one,
since she'd graduated college.

Still, ten years was too much of an age difference for
him to handle. So when she was around he did his best
to keep his mind off sex, difficult as that was sometimes. He rested his elbows on his knees and leaned toward Carl. "Why Erica? Why not someone else?"

"You tell me. Who else could we use?"

He shrugged. "Why not Bonnie?" As far as he was
concerned, his ex and Nick made a perfect couple.

"Why not Bonnie what?"

Adam groaned as Bombshell Bonnie herself filled
the doorway. Dressed in white short shorts, gold high-
heeled sandals and an orange tank top, she looked as if
she was on her way to a job at Hooters instead of her
afternoon traffic report.

"Nothing, darlin'. Adam and I were just talking."

The look she gave Adam could have frozen lava but
he was used to it. "Hello, Bonnie," he said calmly.

As usual, she ignored him. "What's this I hear about
a new promo with Mattress Max?" She perched on the
edge of Carl's desk and leaned toward him, giving him
an eye-level view of her cleavage.

Accustomed to Bonnie's tactics, Carl was unmoved.
"Who told you about that?"

She smoothed her hair back and smiled slyly. "Oh,
a lady never tells."

Carl snorted. "Well, it's nothing to do with you."

"Who's doing the promo?" She looked at Adam. Thank God he wasn't involved in this sleazy scheme. Bonnie didn't need any more reasons to hate him.

"Nick and Erica are doing the promo." Carl turned to the printouts again. "Now if you people don't mind, I have work to do. And so do you two."

Bonnie frowned. "Who's Erica?"

"The production assistant and intern?" Adam stood and joined Bonnie beside Carl's desk. "Erica Gibson."

Bonnie wrinkled her nose as if she'd smelled something nasty. "The one who cussed during the two car dealer ads on air? I thought you fired her."

"Now, Bonnie, everyone deserves a second chance." Carl said mildly.

Adam shifted, remembering the second and third chances Carl had given him. He certainly understood about giving someone the opportunity to redeem herself. "She has a degree in broadcasting from the University of Colorado at Denver," he said.

Bonnie narrowed her eyes. "How do you know so much about her?"

"We've had a few conversations." Not long ones, and Erica did most of the talking, but that was more than Bonnie bothered with. The Bombshell didn't go out of her way for anyone unless she saw some benefit to herself. One of the reasons Adam had split up with her was because he'd been appalled at the way she treated waiters and storeclerks.

Bonnie turned back to Carl. "I have more seniority than any intern. I'm entitled to any special promotion work. Plus our listeners know me."

The thing about Carl was that he looked harmless until crossed. Now he stood and looked Bonnie in the eye, his expression hard and cold. "Last time I checked, my name is on that door over the title Station Manager. So I decide who does the promos and who doesn't."

Bonnie slid off the desk and stood. "Of course you do," she said. "I only thought since I have more experience and the listeners know me—"

"You thought wrong." He glanced at his watch. "Don't you have a traffic report to do in five minutes?"

She pushed her lips out in a pout, but had sense enough not to say anything else. She turned on her heel and left the office with an exaggerated sway of her hips.

When she was gone, Adam turned to Carl again.

"Don't say anything," Carl said without looking up. "Erica's doing the promo and that's that."

Adam knew when he was beaten. Carl hadn't gotten where he was by being a wimp. "All right. But I'm curious. Why didn't you give Bonnie the job? She's popular with the listeners."

Carl's eyes met Adam's, and his mouth twitched in the beginnings of a smile. "Nick refused to work with her."

Adam's eyebrows rose, registering his surprise. He'd have thought Naughty Nick would have been first in line to spend three days in bed with the Bombshell. "Did he say why?"

"He said he didn't want her busting his chops the way she did yours."

"Uh, yeah." He didn't like to be reminded of their very uncordial breakup.

"Hey, listen, I'm not trying to bring up a bad scene, but I don't ever want anything like that happening here again. We got complaint calls for months. I mean, on the air she called you an effing rat b—"

"I know what she called me, Carl." He glanced toward the empty doorway. "It's no secret Bonnie has a bad temper."

"You never should have gotten involved with her."

"I know." He rubbed the back of his neck. "Hey, I was new in town, new to the job. She came on to me and I was flattered. But I've learned my lesson. It won't happen again."

Carl nodded. "One thing I like about you is you're a man who learns from his mistakes." He looked at his watch again.

"I know, I know. I've got a show to do." Adam started to leave, but paused in the doorway. "You'll tell Nick to behave himself with Erica, right?"

"Nick will behave himself. Everything will be great."

Right. Everything would be great. But he was going to worry until this was over with, all the same. He might be unable to do anything about his attraction to Erica, but he hadn't yet found a way to stop thinking about her.

2

"ALL RIGHT, PEEPS. You all know what day it is. That's right—it's Tell All Tuesday. So call me up with your true confessions. Today's topic—your baddest sexcapade. The world and Naughty Nick want to know."

"Sexcapades?" Erica shook her head. This is what she had to look forward to for the next three days—and three nights. The closer it got to the day of her big debut, the longer that seventy-five hours looked. But she'd promised herself she'd see it through. Too many times in her past she'd failed to stick with a plan when the going got tough—hence changing majors three times in college and running through a string of relationships in the past seven years.

But radio was different. This was what she *really* wanted to do, so she was going to make the best of this opportunity. She'd even rehearsed a few comebacks to put Nick in his place. There had to be more than a few women out there who'd cheer to see a player like Nick get his and she planned to use that to her advantage.

Tomorrow was the big day. The past month had flown by in a rush of activity. She'd recorded teasers with Nick that ran throughout the day on the station, posed for photos for billboards and ads, and met with

Mattress Max himself, who'd looked her up and down and announced that plenty of people were sure to stop by to see her in a nightgown.

Great. She studied herself critically in the mirror of the ladies' room at the KROK studios. Last night, on impulse, she'd added a pink streak to her hair. She'd wanted something different to celebrate her public debut. Too bad the debut had to be in bed with Naughty Nick. "It's for a good cause," she reminded herself, and took out a tube of lipstick.

"Hey, Erica."

Erica looked up from freshening her lipstick and was startled to find Bombshell Bonnie talking to her. Before now, Erica would have bet the weather and traffic reporter didn't even know her name. "Uh, hi, Bonnie. How are you?"

"Fine and sassy, as always." She fluffed her blond curls with her fingers and adjusted the straps of the red knit camisole that clung to her curves like a second skin.

"That's good. I'm fine, too." *Not that you asked*. She checked her lipstick in the mirror again.

"Who are you primping for?" Bonnie asked.

"No one." Unfortunately the rush of blood to her face proved her a liar. Actually she'd been hoping to run into Adam. He came in about this time every morning to tape teasers for his afternoon show, to work on any commercial spots he'd been hired for and to pull any songs he wanted that weren't in the scheduled rotation. Ever since she'd been picked for the promo gig with Nick she'd made it a point to be waiting for him, to exchange at least a few words. She was still working on convincing him they could be more than friendly co-workers. She'd decided to take a little more care with her appearance, in hopes of waking him up to the fact that she was a reasonably attractive woman who was, after all, only five years younger than him.

"You're not putting on the glam for Nick, are you?"

Erica was so startled by this suggestion she dropped the tube of lipstick. As she chased it around the sink, she shook her head violently. "Nick! No way. What made you think that?"

"You're doing that furniture store promo with him tomorrow aren't you? I thought you might be trying to butter him up so he'd throw some more work your way. Maybe make you a regular part of his show."

She stared at Bonnie. "But Nick's show is all about him being a player. Having a female sidekick wouldn't fit very well with that." Except for the times when they had to be together to do promo stuff, she'd made it a point to avoid Nick. He'd made a few suggestive comments on his show but then, Nick was always making suggestive comments. It was part of his whole shtick.

Bonnie narrowed her eyes. "Since when does anything in this business make sense?" She tapped Erica on the shoulder. "Us girls have to stick together. And we do whatever it takes to get ahead, right?"

"Uh, right." Except that she couldn't see herself posing for *Playboy* anytime soon. Or going after Nick Cassidy. Ick!

Bonnie smiled. "That's right. You just remember that."

"I will. I better get back to work." Erica was already late for her chat with Adam.

He was coming up the stairs from the basement as she was descending. Man, he was hot! While most jocks were behind a microphone instead of in front of a camera for a reason, Adam had a rugged, outdoorsy look that was definitely easy on the eyes. "Hi, Adam." She flashed him her warmest smile.

"Hey, Erica. How's it going?"

"Great. Everything's set for my big debut tomorrow." She wasn't counting her ill-fated intro of the car dealer ads. That was a last-minute fill-in. This was her real chance to star.

"What's with the pink?" He gestured toward her hair.

She put one hand to her shoulder-length locks. "Just something fun I did, something different for my debut."

He nodded. "Looks good. Hey, I saw the new billboards for the furniture store promo," he said. "That's a good picture of you."

"You think so?" She flushed, pleased that he'd noticed. She'd seen the ads for the first time that morning and had almost run off the road. The first ads had referred to her only as Nick's "mystery woman" but these new spots had her picture as well. There was something disconcerting about seeing her face twenty feet high looming over the roadway.

"Yeah. Too bad Nick's ugly mug was spoiling the picture."

She laughed. "Not everyone can be as good-looking as you are," she teased.

He looked away from her and cleared his throat. "Uh, yeah. I shouldn't·be so harsh on Nick."

"What's on the schedule for your show this afternoon?" she asked, anxious to keep the conversation going.

"It's Friday, so we have the trivia contest."

Adam was the station's rock trivia expert. Every Friday listeners had the chance to stump him with questions. Winners earned cool prizes.

"Nickelback's doing a live performance at two to promote their concert tonight at the Pepsi Center," he continued. "We're giving away tickets."

"Are you going?"

"No, Nick is doing that one. We'll have the station trailer set up and he'll be giving away swag before the show, then he'll take the winners of the drawing for backstage passes to meet the band."

"He'll be a bear in the morning, then. He hates those late nights."

"That's life in the radio biz." He glanced her way again. "Maybe you want to rethink your career."

She shook her head. "No. This is what I really want to do. When I was little, other kids played CDs—I had to put on a whole show, with commercials and everything."

"I used to do that, too. I'd forgotten all that until now." His watch beeped and he glanced at it. "I have to go now. It was good talking to you."

"It's always good talking to you, Adam." She tried to put a little extra sultriness into the words, but he'd already turned away and was heading up the stairs, two at a time.

She sighed. Her seductress skills definitely needed work.

On the way to her cubicle, she stopped to talk to her

best friend at the station, the production secretary, Tanisha. "How long have you worked here, Tanisha?" she asked.

"Fourteen months, twenty-two days and six hours. But who's counting? Why?"

"I was just wondering. Do you know if Adam Hawkins has dated anybody since Bonnie?"

"Mr. Handsome Hawk hasn't dated much of anyone since the Bombshell exploded," she said. "Of course, with Carl's rule against the on-air personalities dating, he'd almost have to find a girlfriend outside of work. But I haven't heard about anyone." She grinned. "And I make it my business to keep up on all the gossip."

"That's interesting."

"I saw you two talking together just now. That's more words than I've seen him exchange with anyone in months."

"It took me weeks to get him to say even that much to me." A man who kept his emotions reined in so tightly must have all kinds of passions bottled up inside, just waiting for the right woman to unleash them.

Of course, she could be all wrong. Maybe Adam was horribly repressed and not the demonstrative type. But she'd love the chance to find out.

"So are you interested in him?" Tanisha asked.

She checked to make sure they were alone, then leaned closer to Tanisha. "Let's just say I could be."

"Well good luck. He's a tough one to figure. I mean, we know he's not gay, we're pretty sure he's available, but *why* is he available?"

"Maybe Bonnie broke his heart."

"Hmmph." Tanisha sniffed. "I was here the day it all

went down. He's the one who tried to break up with her. I don't think he was all that sad to see the back of her."

"Then I'd say it was time for a new woman in his life."

"But how are you going to get around Carl?"

"I'm not on-air talent, remember? This promo thing is just a temporary assignment."

Tanisha laughed. "You go. Of course, you might have to fight off Naughty Nick first."

She made a face. "Don't remind me."

"I don't envy you three days in bed with that octopus."

"I'm thinking about arming myself with Mace and a stun gun. Think that would stop him?"

"Better bring some earplugs, too. I never met a man who liked to talk so much—about himself."

"Earplugs. Gotcha." She mentally added these to her list. This was going to be the longest seventy-five hours of her life, but she was going to make the most of the time. By the time it was over she'd have a gig as the station's newest jock and Naughty Nick would have learned to keep his hands to himself.

BONNIE GLARED at the billboard looming over the Englewood Light Rail Station. Five years she'd been with KROK and her face had never been on a billboard. Little Miss Muffet had worked there a lousy six months and her simpering mug was plastered all over town. Bonnie kicked the curb. So much for thinking seniority counted for anything.

She'd been sure she was on her way when she'd latched onto Adam Hawkins. Not only was the Hawk the best-looking thing to cross the threshold of KROK in years, he was a genuinely nice guy. Which to her meant he was easily manipulated. She'd smiled and flirted and before she knew it, he was following her home. She figured in a matter of weeks she'd be sitting behind a control board, doing the afternoon show with him. A few months after that, she'd find a way to lose him and she'd have a solo gig.

But when she'd suggested she sit in on a few shows with him, he'd turned her down cold. He didn't want to muddle things by mixing business with pleasure, he'd said.

He didn't want to share the spotlight with anyone else was the problem. She'd figured she could change his mind, and then he'd had the nerve to dump her. And right before his show, too!

Well, she'd shown him. When it was time to do her traffic report, she'd lit into him. She'd shown the world what a lousy bastard he was.

And then Carl had to come unglued. He'd totally overreacted. He'd even called her unprofessional. And Adam got off scot-free. It figured. Men got all the breaks in this business.

She scowled up at the billboard again. Carl was still holding that little outburst with Adam against her. Otherwise why would he have agreed to let a nobody like that do a major promo? And a sexy one at that? What was sexy about a kid like her? Everybody knew Bombshell Bonnie was, well, a bombshell.

Sometimes Carl could be so dumb. The light rail train pulled into the station and she took a last look at the billboard before climbing onto the car. Everybody

at KROK was dumb if they thought she was giving up
that easily. She was going to have her own show there
sooner or later. All she needed was the right opportunity, and the right person to help her get there.

"IT'S WET and nasty out there tonight. A band of thun-
derstorms stretching from the eastern plains into the
foothills has traffic snarled all over town. Wrecks working at C-470 and Broadway, westbound Six and Sheri-
dan, northbound I-225 and Parker. Slow and go around
the Pepsi Center. And we can expect much the same
story for the rest of the week."

Adam inched his Jeep along C-470 toward his home
in Morrison, just southwest of Denver. Thank God he
hadn't drawn the Pepsi Center gig. Pulling the station
trailer would be a nightmare in this weather.

Three more miles to his exit and it was taking forever to get there. His car stopped again almost directly
under a KROK billboard. Erica smiled down on him,
posed with Nick in front of an enormous brass bed.

For probably the thousandth time, he wished she
didn't work for the radio station. Why couldn't she be
a schoolteacher or a secretary or an attorney or anything
but a co-worker? If he didn't have to work with her, he
might risk asking her out. Yeah, the age thing made him
feel like a dirty old man, but he'd risk it to find out if
she was as hot in real life as she was in his fantasies.

But she did work for KROK, so no dice. Maybe she
didn't technically fall under Carl's rule, but Adam had
learned the hard way to keep his work life and his personal life separate. There was too much potential for
major damage if they mingled. He'd caught himself ra-

tionalizing why this time would be different, but he'd resolutely shoved the thoughts away. He wasn't going to make the mistake of thinking with his cock, the way he had with Bonnie.

Of course, Erica was young. She hadn't screwed up her life the way he had. More than once lately he'd sensed that she was doing her best to let him know she was interested in him. He was flattered, and he'd thought about trying to explain what had happened with Bonnie, and how close he'd come to losing his job after their big bust-up. How he couldn't afford to mess up again. He wanted her to understand he wasn't rejecting her, just trying to keep them both out of trouble.

But he'd never found the right words to say all that. He always got too caught up in listening to her, in watching the way her eyes lit up when she was excited about something, and enjoying the way he felt when she smiled at him.

And now for the next three days she'd be sharing that bed with Nick. Of course, they wouldn't be doing anything. For one thing, even at night there were security guards and cameras everywhere. But still, the thought was unsettling.

He supposed he could hope for a flood to wash out the Furniture Gallery and make the whole bed-in thing impossible. The way the skies had opened up, it was a remote possibility.

"Naughty Nick here, reminding you that starting tomorrow, I'll be broadcasting live from the showroom of Mattress Max's Furniture Gallery, Wadsworth and East Six. Stop by and see me and my lovely sidekick, Erica, as we begin our seventy-five hour bed-in to raise money for the Salvation Army's new homeless shelter. Bring your donation by in person. And give me your ideas for what you'd do if you had seventy-five hours to spend in bed with a good-looking co-worker."

He punched off the radio and glared up at the billboard again. It was going to be a very long three days.

RED FLANNEL pajamas with cartoon puppy dogs all over them—check. Red fuzzy slippers—check. Teddy bear— check. Sleep mask—check. Earplugs—check. Toiletries, throat lozenges, water bottle, makeup, clean underwear—check. Civilian clothes to wear home— check. Erica zipped the duffel and dragged it toward her car. She had twenty minutes to make it to Mattress Max's, ten minutes to change once she got there and no time at all to calm down and convince herself that she was, absolutely, doing the right thing.

At least there was no traffic this time of morning, and the rain had stopped for a while. She raced her neon-green Volkswagen up the entrance ramp to Interstate 70 and headed toward the Furniture Gallery. She hadn't slept much the night before, having been tortured by doubt and by erotic dreams starring Adam. Too bad he wasn't her partner in this crazy promo. She'd have definitely found something sexier to wear for him, and would have done her best to make sure she didn't have to wear it very long once the lights went out.

Though the surrounding businesses were dark, Mattress Max's Furniture Gallery was lit up like a fairgrounds. She spotted the KROK production van near the front door. Mason, a production tech, waved at her as she drove past and parked the VW around back.

Then she grabbed her bag and raced toward the private rest room that had been set aside for her and Nick to share. It was Mattress Max's executive washroom, complete with shower. Fortunately Max himself wasn't there this time of morning, so she didn't have to deal with him.

Nick was nowhere in sight, either. She changed into the flannel pjs, already rehearsing the speech she'd prepared for Carl, who was sure to complain. Her angle was that showing less skin was actually more enticing, because it left things to the imagination. Plus, she'd noticed before that the furniture showroom tended to be cold. He wouldn't want her getting sick, would he?

She didn't really expect him to buy it, but she had to try. She would compromise with a KROK T-shirt and boxers, but she drew the line at Victoria's Secret or Fredericks's.

Carl had explained everything to her multiple times—the remote mini-transmitter on the truck would send the signal to the transmitter at the studio for broadcast. A board op there would run the production board during the morning show, with the regular staff taking over at nine o'clock. The main thing she and Nick had to do was listen for their on-air cues.

The production crew had been busy, setting up the mics and other equipment around the bed. It was some bed, too—a king-size brass number with a fake mink spread and blue satin sheets. Half a dozen of the fluffiest pillows she'd ever laid eyes on were piled at the head, and twin black lacquer nightstands were already stocked with water, tissues and matching brass lamps.

"Erica! There you are." Carl spotted her and hurried

over. He frowned at the pajamas. "Puppy dogs? You couldn't come up with anything better than that?"

"I didn't want to be cold." She hugged her arms over her chest.

He shook his head. "That's the least of my worries right now. Here, you go ahead and get into bed." He escorted her to her home away from home for the next three days. "We'll get started in a minute here."

"Sound checks out okay, Carl."

The familiar voice sent a warm tingle through her and she froze in the act of climbing into bed and stared at the man who'd appeared on the other side. "Adam? What are you doing here?"

"Morning, Erica." He cut his eyes to the station manager. "Didn't Carl tell you?"

"Tell me what?"

Carl coughed. "Nick was in a car accident on the way home from the Pepsi Center last night. He's going to be all right, but he'll be out of commission for a while, so Adam is filling in."

She turned to Adam again. For the first time she noticed that below the KROK T-shirt, he was wearing blue plaid pajama bottoms. A warm glow settled over her and she couldn't hold back a smile. "That's great! I mean, that's really nice of you."

"In the bed, both of you," Carl said. "We're almost ready to go live."

They each turned back the covers and settled awkwardly on either side of the bed, careful not to touch. "You ready?" Adam asked.

She took a deep breath, immediately aware of the scent of his aftershave and the underlying aroma of him. Her stomach fluttered. "I guess so." No way was she going to screw up this time. "Are you?"

Worry lines fanned out from his eyes, but he nodded. "I guess so. It's been a while, but I think I remember how."

She gasped. Wow, get the man in bed and he turned into a completely different person. "It's been a while?"

"Yeah, I used to do a morning show in Carmel, but that was years ago. I hope my mouth still works in the morning."

"Oh. Oh, I'm sure it will." She pulled the covers up a little more, hoping he'd been too busy setting up the equipment to notice her grinning. It was all she could do not to pump her fist and shout out "Yes!" She couldn't believe she was here. In bed. With Adam Hawkins.

She watched him out of the corner of her eye as he settled his earphones into place and adjusted the microphone. What had Bonnie said about taking advantage of every opportunity? Well here was a golden one to let Adam know exactly what she thought of him.

A lot could happen in three days, couldn't it?

3

"THIS IS THE HAWK coming to you live from a king-size bed in the middle of Mattress Max's Furniture Gallery." Adam tried to get comfortable in the big bed, despite the distraction of the woman beside him. He nodded to her, her cue to get ready for her morning show debut. "With me is the ever-effervescent Erica."

"Good morning, everyone." Erica smiled into the mic, living up to the nickname he'd just saddled her with. *Did she always look this good at a little after six in the morning? And since when had flannel been so sexy?*

"We know you were expecting Naughty Nick," she continued. "But unfortunately, he couldn't be with us this morning."

"Just as well," Adam said. "I'm not into threesomes myself." *Aaargh. Where had that come from? This was not the time for sexual wordplay.* "Seriously, folks, Nick was injured last night in a traffic accident on the way home from the Pepsi Center concert. The last report we had he'd just come out of surgery and was doing well. We wish him a speedy recovery."

"That's right, Nick. Get well soon." Erica's eyes lit with mischief. "Meanwhile, I'm going to do my best to make do with the Hawk here."

"Make do? Woman, that is harsh. I'm wounded."
Was she really disappointed to be spending the next
three days with him instead of Nick?

She laughed and sat cross-legged in the bed, her
knee brushing his. "I don't know. Are you really an
early-morning kind of guy?"

You'd think in a king-size bed they could avoid contact. He moved over a little. "Every man is an early
morning kind of guy. Didn't you know that?" There he
went with the double entendres again. Was it his years
in rock radio, or merely the fact that he couldn't stop
thinking about sex around her?

"And I thought Nick was going to be a handful."

And just what did she think her hands were going to
be full of? He dropped his voice to a seductive rumble.
"Don't think you're up to spending three days in bed
with me?"

The look she sent him made his temperature climb.
"The question ought to be, is the Hawk ready to spend
three days in bed with *me?*"

No. Yes. Would he really last three days? Considering the heat they'd generated in less than ten minutes
he was liable to self-combust long before their seventy-five hour deadline was met.

He adjusted the microphone on his headset. "That
sounded like a challenge to me, folks. Did it to you?
Come on down to the Furniture Gallery and place your
bets."

"I think you mean make your donations."

"You use your terminology, I'll stick to mine."

"However you put it, the bottom line is we're here
raising money for the Salvation Army's new homeless

shelter," she said. "Stop by and add your cash or check to our collection bin. And while you're at it, add your get-well wishes to the giant card we've posted for Nick."

"For those of you still lazing around in *your* beds, here's a little rock and roll to get you going."

As the music started, Erica ripped off her headset and leaned back against the pillows. "How'd I do?" she asked.

"You sound like a pro." And she looked almost too tempting, half-reclining in the bed, her hair spread out on the pillow behind her. He swallowed hard and looked away, attempting to focus on the few Furniture Gallery employees who'd started to gather. "I still can't believe Carl agreed to this. How can anybody spend three days in a bed?"

"Oh, I don't know. Maybe under the right circumstances. With the right person."

There was a definite seductive purr in her voice. Was *he* the right person she wouldn't mind in her bed?

"We get to take breaks," she said. "I mean, you can get up and walk around."

"Right. To go to the john. I guess I ought to be grateful for that."

She stretched her arms over her head, a movement that brought her breasts into sharper focus against the flannel. "Well, I'm going to find a way to have a good time with this. I mean, how many people get paid to basically have fun in bed?"

There his mind went again, reading more into her words than she probably meant. He could certainly think of a few ways to have fun with her in bed…. He tried looking away again, but his gaze insisted on wandering back to her. She was unbuttoning her top now. "What are you doing?" he asked, alarmed.

"It's a lot warmer in here than I thought." She stripped off the shirt and tossed it aside, revealing a red tank top underneath.

Only when his vision blurred did he realize he'd stopped breathing. He turned his back to her. "Can we get some coffee over here? And some ice water." If all else failed, he could dump the water in his lap.

"That was Maroon 5 with 'This Love,'" she said, right on cue. "If you're on your way into work this morning, stop by and say hi. The Hawk and I are broadcasting from Mattress Max's Furniture Gallery at East Six and Wadsworth."

"If you bring us a donation this morning, we've got free T-shirts and CDs to give away." Adam checked his clipboard and saw that it was time for a plug for Mattress Max. "And while you're here, try out Max's own line of Therapedic bedding—the most comfortable mattress you'll find anywhere."

"This one certainly is comfortable." Erica bounced up and down and grinned at him.

He couldn't help but notice that the mattress wasn't the only thing bouncing, and almost forgot his lines. The engineer hissed in his earphones, reminding him to avoid the broadcasting sin of dead air. He forced himself to focus on the clipboard. "Max is running a special right now. Buy a mattress during the K-Rock bed-in and he'll throw in a frame and two Therapedic pillows absolutely free."

"The pillows are definitely very comfy." She smiled

at him and beads of sweat popped out on his forehead. He'd have to talk to someone about getting a fan or something.

Was she deliberately flirting with him? Maybe she thought that was what was expected of her. Later, when they were off the air, he'd explain to her that she didn't have to act that way with him. He wasn't Naughty Nick. They would just do the show the way he always did, ask for donations and forget about all the flirting and sexy talk.

If only he could convince his body to do the same.

At 9:00 the morning show ended and Erica and Adam were off the air. Now their job was to talk to the people who stopped by to donate, take turns answering the phones for people who wanted to make pledges, and do the occasional live call-in throughout the day.

In between times they were free to take a break to eat or freshen up in the bathroom, though they weren't supposed to get too far from the bed.

Erica watched as Adam signed autographs for a trio of smiling women. She didn't really blame them for smiling. Dressed in rumpled pajamas, his hair tousled, he looked like a man who'd just rolled out of bed. And one who hadn't spent his time there working *or* sleeping.

Flirting with him had come naturally. But then she'd decided to try turning up the heat a notch. Why not? There was no way he could pretend she was just another co-worker when they were so close together—both in nightclothes and in a bed. Why not take advantage of that to let him know how she really felt? And if she was lucky, one thing might lead to another and they'd never be "just friends" again.

She was busy reviewing the schedule on the clipboard when Carl stopped by. "How's it going?" he asked.

"Good. How did I sound?"

"Great. You got everything you need here?"

Adam turned away from his admirers and joined them. "We could use a fan," he said. "It's too warm in here."

Carl looked at Erica. "She said she was cold earlier."

She coughed, recalling the excuse she'd made up for wearing the flannel. She wished now she'd packed sexier clothes. She'd had to settle for the tank top but it had served the purpose and gotten Adam's attention. "I'm fine now," she said.

"You did good," he said again. "Keep it up. I like the sexy stuff. The listeners love it, too."

Adam frowned. "About the sexy stuff," he said. "Nick's not here, so we don't have to do that."

"Didn't you hear me?" Carl said. "I said keep it up. Besides, you two sounded like you were having fun."

Adam shifted from one foot to the other, avoiding looking at Erica. "Sure. I just don't want people to get the wrong idea."

She laughed. "Don't worry about me. And hey, maybe my reputation could use a little spicing up."

"Great. Now some big bruiser of a boyfriend will come looking for me with a baseball bat."

"Don't worry. I don't have a boyfriend—big bruiser or not."

"Then see, no problem," Carl said. "Have fun with it. But not too much fun."

She made a face at him. "Aren't you the spoilsport."

"There's security cameras all over the place." He pointed to opaque plastic domes in the ceiling. There was one directly over the bed. "They'll record everything you do."

"Everything?" So much for her plans to seduce Adam.

He winked. "Everything."

"Thanks for the warning," Adam said. "But it wasn't necessary. Erica and I are professionals."

"Yeah, well last time I looked you were a man and a woman, too."

Adam's frown was a real scowl now. "I won't get out of line."

Carl shrugged. "I didn't say anything, did I?"

Had they forgotten she was here? What if *she* wanted to get out of line? "How's Nick?" she asked, anxious to change the subject.

"Okay. I saw him after he came out of surgery. They had him on a morphine pump and he was feeling no pain. He's got a pin in his leg and a cast up to his thigh, and his shoulder's all bandaged up." He wiped his face with an oversize green bandanna. "He's lucky he wasn't killed."

"Poor guy." She shuddered. "Funny how a few minutes can change everything, isn't it?"

"Yeah." Adam was looking at her. Was he thinking about how this changed things between them, too?

"Now get back in bed." Carl shooed them toward the bed. "We want some photos for the Web site."

She settled back against the pillows beside Adam, smiling for the camera, all her senses focused on the man beside her. They were almost touching, but not quite, the satin sheets bunched up between them.

"No, no, no. Act like you like each other." Carl stood beside the cameraman, motioning for them to move closer together. "This is supposed to be sexy. Attention-getting. You're having a good time, remember? It's for a good cause."

She glanced at Adam, who wore a pained expression. "Carl, I—" he began.

She couldn't decide if he was shy or simply had an overdeveloped sense of propriety. She absolutely refused to consider that he might not *want* to get closer to her. She couldn't be that far off in reading the signals he was sending out when no one else was around.

Fine, then. She'd be happy to help things along a little. She pulled the sheets from around them and slid closer, her hip snugged up against his, his arm brushing the side of her breast. "How's this?" she asked, and threw both arms around him.

"Great! Great! Adam, put your arm around her. That's it. Now big smiles!"

The flash blinded them, but it did nothing to dim her awareness of Adam's arm around her or the warmth of his body against hers. He'd gotten over his reluctance quickly enough, his fingers kneading her waist, his body angling toward hers slightly. Only a half-turn and they'd be facing each other, looking into each other's eyes, their lips almost touching....

"That's great. You look hot. We'll get a million hits on the Web site with these."

"I think a million's a little optimistic," Adam said,

his arm still wrapped around her. "It's not the Paris Hilton video."

"Now there's an idea." Carl's eyes took on a wicked gleam. "Video. I'll have to talk with the Web designer about that."

"Hey, Adam, come over here and check this schedule, will you?" their production assistant, Mason, called.

Did she imagine his reluctance to pull away from her? She hugged a pillow to her chest and watched him climb out of bed and cross the floor to speak with Mason. Obviously Adam had enjoyed the cuddling as much as she had. If she could only figure out a way for them to enjoy it when no one was looking…no one but all those security cameras.

She glanced up at the smoked plastic dome. Was there someone sitting at a console somewhere, monitoring them right now? She stuck out her tongue just in case. That's what they got for spoiling her fun. Wonder if she could cover them with a sheet…?

"What are you looking at?"

She started as he joined her in the bed once more. "I'm thinking how boring it must be for whoever monitors those cameras," she said.

"This is probably more exciting than staring at screens full of furniture all day, which is what they usually do."

She laughed. "So far it's been fun."

His eyes caught hers and lingered. "Yeah. It has been fun."

There was no time for further conversation, as Adam was called on to do a public service announcement for the Salvation Army and Erica did a quick interview with the entertainment columnist for the *Post*. The rest of the day was a blur of talking with fans, posing for photos, signing autographs and making regular on-air appeals for more donations. Before she knew it, they were well into the afternoon.

"Time to do a call-in, folks." Mason held out their headsets and motioned for them to get ready.

"How are you two doing out there?" Audra's voice came through loud and clear. "No napping on the job, now."

"Nobody told *me* that," Erica said. "I was hoping to catch up on my beauty sleep."

"She doesn't need it, folks, trust me," Adam said.

She gave him her most killer smile. Maybe she'd been wrong about him not seeing her as an available woman. He didn't seem to be having that problem now.

"We've raised over two thousand dollars in our first eight hours," Adam said. "Let's double that by nine when we say good-night."

After-work traffic brought a rush of donations and visitors. For a few minutes, Erica even had a line of people waiting for her autograph. Talk about a rush. "I could get used to this celebrity business," she told Adam when the crowd had dwindled.

"You're a natural at it."

A little after nine the production crew packed up for the day. Someone delivered a take-out pizza and checked that they had everything they needed and then everyone left. Finally they were alone. After the hubbub of the day, the quiet was a little unsettling.

"I don't know about you, but I'm not messing up the

sheets with pizza sauce." Adam moved into a nearby leather recliner.

"Right." She pulled up an armchair next to him and helped herself to a slice of pizza. "I'm starved. That burger I wolfed down at lunch is long gone."

"Tomorrow we lobby for more snacks." He wiped his fingers with a fistful of napkins. "After all, we've got to keep our strength up."

"Yes, it's such strenuous work." Maybe not physically, but she had to admit, being "on" for so many hours was exhausting.

"The first day went pretty well, I thought," Adam said. "Tomorrow shouldn't be as hectic."

"It went great." But there was still the first night to get through. What would happen then? She had a lot of fantasies about what she'd *like* to happen, but the security cameras had ruined all that. So how would she and Adam handle spending the night in the same bed?

"I wonder how Nick's feeling about now?" Adam asked.

"Probably not so good." She had a sudden image of Nick in a hospital gown and quickly shoved it aside. Some things she did not want to see. "I'm sorry he was hurt, but I'm glad I'm doing this promo with you instead of him."

"Oh, Nick's all right. Most of his rep is just part of his act." He glanced at her. "I'm sure he would have been a perfect gentleman."

And will you *be a perfect gentleman?* She hoped not. She was beginning to worry that he wasn't attracted to her at all. She wasn't a bombshell like Bonnie, but she'd never had reason to worry about her looks much before. Who would have guessed her dream job would be so hard on her ego?

Suddenly she had to get away from him, if only for a few minutes. She yawned. "I'm wiped."

"Yeah." He set the pizza box aside. "It's getting late and we've got another early morning tomorrow."

"At least we don't have a long commute." She stood and began gathering up their paper plates and cups.

"I'll do that." He took the trash from her, his hand grazing hers, sending a rush of heat through her. "You can have the bathroom first to get ready to turn in."

"Thanks." She grabbed up her duffel and made her way through the darkened furniture displays toward the bathroom. Minus the piped-in music and crowds of shoppers, this part of the store was downright creepy. A display of lamps cast long shadows across the floor and an overstuffed chair loomed like a crouching beast. She hurried to the bathroom and hummed to herself while she washed her face and brushed her teeth, then raced back to the bed, grateful for Adam's solid presence.

While he took his turn in the bathroom, she snuggled under the covers. The bedside lamps cast pools of golden light across the bed, making it a cozy island in the surrounding darkness. Whereas the silence had seemed unnatural in the rest of the store, their luxurious display seemed peaceful.

She settled back against the pillows and gazed into the darkness, letting the quiet wash over her. How odd to be here, in what was a somewhat impossible situation. And yet, how wonderful it all was too. At that moment, she wouldn't have traded places with anyone.

Then she heard Adam's footsteps approaching, the heels of his slippers slapping on the tile showroom floor. He stepped into the pool of light, looking larger than he had before, and smelling of herbal soap. Her stomach gave a nervous shimmy, but she forced a smile and patted the covers beside her. "Come on in. It's very cozy."

He avoided looking at her, but turned back the covers and climbed in, reaching over to switch off the lamp on his side. She turned off her lamp also, and lay back in the darkness, aware of the weight of him beside her, the bed creaking and covers shifting as he made himself comfortable.

"I hope you don't snore," she said, her tone teasing.

"I don't think so," he said. "No one's ever complained before."

"Oh. Have there been a lot of someones?" The darkness made her bold.

Silence stretched between them and she was afraid she'd gone too far. She turned toward him, barely making out his silhouette in the darkness. He cleared his throat. "Not that many. You?"

She shook her head, then realized he couldn't see her. "Not many." Six actually, but she wasn't going to tell him that.

"Oh. Um, just so you know, I, um…"

She held her breath, waiting for him to finish the sentence. He sounded so serious, as if he was about to confess something important—maybe his real feelings for her?

"Never mind. It's not important. Good night." He rolled over, his back to her.

She stared at him, tempted to grab one of the pillows and whomp him over the head with it. But a pillow wasn't hard enough to knock any real sense into him. Besides, getting into a fight their first night wasn't going to make the next two days any easier.

She sighed and turned her back to him. She shut her eyes tight and willed herself to breathe more slowly, faking sleep. She doubted she'd get any rest, but the exhaustion of the day got the better of her. Before she knew it, her body relaxed and she drifted off.

ADAM WAS DREAMING, one of those amazing erotic dreams from which he never wanted to wake. He was with a woman, of course, a warm, soft woman. His hands embraced her firm breasts and her bottom was cradled against his erection. She smelled like sweet flowers and her hair felt like silk against his face. He didn't know who she was, but he didn't particularly care. She was a dream woman, a product of his imagination.

The fact that he realized this told him he wasn't too deeply into the dream. In fact, he could feel morning tugging at him, pulling him from sleep, but he resisted, holding on to the woman. He had to hand it to his subconscious—it had conjured up an amazing fantasy female this time. She made a little moaning sound and snuggled closer, sharpening his arousal. He caught his breath as her nipple hardened and pressed against his palm. He buried his face in her neck, his lips against her hot, smooth skin as he thrust against her. He wished she'd turn over. In a minute, he'd see if he could manage it, but the trouble with dreams was that it wasn't always easy to move, especially when he was so close to waking.

He shifted his hand to her waist, across the curve of her hip, pressing down. Obligingly she rolled onto her back, flipping onto her side to face him. Her arms slipped around him and for the first time he registered that she was wearing clothes, the soft cotton of her pajamas brushing against him.

Eyes still shut tight, he frowned. Since when did his dream fantasies wear clothes? And pajamas at that. If anything, this woman ought to be wearing some silky negligee. Or better yet, nothing at all.

He tugged at the edge of the pajama top, determined to remedy this matter. Obviously his subconscious wanted to make fulfilling this fantasy more challenging.

She was kissing him now, tracing the line of his jaw with her tongue. He groaned, trying to hold back the wakefulness stealing over him. Just a little longer. At least until he got her undressed and he was inside her...

Noises disrupted his concentration—footsteps, the clang of metal, distant voices drawing nearer. He winced against a sudden flare of light against his closed eyelids and groaned. Not yet. Only a few minutes more...

The dream woman gave a small squeal and shoved away from him, even as he tried to hold her.

"Adam, what the hell do you think you're doing?"

The words jerked him awake more effectively than a bucket of ice water. He opened his eyes, squinting against the glare of bright overhead lights, and stared into the frowning face of the station manager, Carl.

"What the hell do you think you're doing?" Carl asked again.

4

"NOTHING." Adam rolled away from Erica and sat up. "We weren't doing anything." He slid his gaze to his bed partner. She was sitting up, too, the covers tucked up under her breasts.

The breasts that had been pressed again his chest seconds ago, so warm and soft…

He swallowed a groan and looked at Carl again. He couldn't say the sight made him feel any better. His boss was frowning, his bottom lip jutted out.

"Are you sure it was nothing?" Carl directed the question at Erica. "You two looked pretty cozy just now."

Erica smiled. Except for the heightened flush of her cheeks, she didn't give away that anything out of the ordinary had happened. How was it someone who had just awakened could look so dazzling? "Don't be silly, Carl. We're both still fully clothed, aren't we?"

He could think of a lot of not-so-innocent things they could do that wouldn't require them to get undressed, but now wasn't the time to mention them. And as long as they worked together, there wouldn't be a time to mention them.

"See that you stay that way," Carl grumped.

She turned toward Adam and looked at him through lowered lashes. "Adam's been a perfect gentleman," she said.

Right. A perfect gentleman with an incredible hard-on.

Carl looked unconvinced, but he didn't protest. "I came by to give you some good news."

"What's that?" Adam asked. Were they going to end this silly stunt before it got out of hand? Not that it was exactly under control at the moment.

"Mattress Max likes what you're doing so much that he's pledged to donate ten thousand dollars to the Salvation Army for their shelter."

"That's fantastic." Erica wrapped her arms around her knees and grinned. "That will almost double the money we've raised."

"The money isn't ours—or rather the Salvation Army's—yet," Carl said. "Max won't pay it unless you stay here the full seventy-five hours. Until Monday at 9:00 a.m."

"That shouldn't be a problem." She turned to Adam. "We can do it, can't we?"

"Yeah, sure." He tried to inject a little more cheerfulness into his voice. "We're barely getting started here."

Carl stepped back, and shoved his hands in his pockets. "All right, then. You can announce the offer on the air during your show. It should pump up the excitement a little. We don't want things to start getting too dull."

"I'm certainly not bored," Erica said.

"Me, neither." He was horny, frustrated, sleep-deprived and aggravated, but he wasn't bored.

"I'd better go freshen up before the show starts."

Both men watched as she climbed out of bed and picked up her duffel. "I'll be right back," she said.

When she was gone, Carl's scowl returned. "Don't forget this place is full of cameras," he said.

"I know."

"I don't want any trouble."

Adam resented the implication that he was a troublemaker. "You're the one who came up with this crazy stunt."

"And you're the one being paid to do a good job."

"Don't worry." He threw back the covers and sat up on the side of the bed. "I know how to do my job."

"Good. You're on in forty-five minutes."

Forty-five minutes. Right. Forty-five minutes before he climbed back into this bed with Ms. Irresistible. Erica better hurry up and let him have his turn in the shower. He needed it—with the water turned on cold.

Carl left and Adam grabbed the clipboard and pretended to study the morning's play list. But the song titles scarcely registered. Why had he groped Erica in his sleep? Sure, any breathing, straight man would be attracted to her, but he'd thought he had better self-control than that. After all, he'd been in tougher spots before.

All the years he'd spent avoiding trouble ought to come in handy now. Erica was just a challenge of a different kind.

ERICA COMBED through her freshly washed hair and stared at her reflection in the bathroom mirror. How was she ever going to go back out there and not let on to everyone how she was feeling?

She couldn't keep back a grin. Laughing out loud, she hugged herself and did a victory dance around the small room. Yes! Adam might treat her like his little sister in public, but last night—or rather, this morning—had proved his true feelings were anything but brotherly.

If only Carl hadn't come along and interrupted what could have been a really amazing moment. If they'd been alone and Adam had awakened to find her in his arms, would he have been so quick to pull away?

She opened her duffel and pulled out a KROK T-shirt and a pair of baggy blue boxers. Her smile faded as she studied the outfit she'd intended to throw Naughty Nick off the track. Not exactly come-hither couture.

She slumped onto the toilet and considered her options. If she wanted to build on the attraction Adam had revealed during sleep, she needed something that would catch him off guard again.

Everybody knew that men were visual creatures, turned on by what they saw. She needed to give Adam a real eyeful. Make herself irresistible.

She frowned at the clothing wadded in her hand. Boxers and a T-shirt weren't going to cut it.

She looked around the bathroom, hoping for inspiration, but short of fashioning a toga out of the bath towel, she didn't have any ideas.

Time to call for reinforcements. She dug in her bag for her cell phone and punched in a number.

"Hello?" The voice on the other end of the line was groggy.

"Tanisha, this is Erica. I need your help."

"Isn't it a little early in the morning to sound so desperate?" Tanisha yawned. "I wouldn't have thought laying around in bed with the Handsome Hawk would be that difficult."

"Oh, that's not the problem. Not really."

"So how is it? Did the two of you get to know each other better when the lights went out?"

She blushed. As far as she was concerned, she and Adam hadn't gotten to know each other nearly well enough yet. "That's what I need a little help with."

"Thanks, but I'm not into threesomes."

"Very funny. I'm serious here. I thought I was going to be doing this gig with Nick, not Adam. I didn't exactly come prepared."

"You want me to bring you a box of condoms or something?"

"Tanisha!" She almost dropped the phone.

"Well, what am I supposed to think when you say you're not prepared?"

"I meant I don't have the right clothes. All I brought to wear was flannel pajamas, boxer shorts and T-shirts."

"Yeah, not exactly clothes that say seduction is on the menu. Fortunately today is your lucky day."

"Oh?"

"You look like you wear the same size as me. And I happen to have a dresser full of killer lingerie. Guaranteed to have any man worshipping at your feet."

Heat curled through her at the image of Adam on his knees before her. "Help me out and I'll buy you the biggest box of Godiva chocolates you ever saw," she said.

Tanisha laughed. "It's a deal. I'll see you after the morning show."

"Thanks. I owe you."

"I want all the details later."

"You bet." She hung up the phone and replaced it in her bag, then turned to the mirror once more. Right now she looked like a refugee from a teen slumber party, but in a few hours she'd be dressed for battle.

Adam didn't stand a chance.

BY THE END of the morning show, Adam was feeling better about the situation with Erica. Yes, she was an attractive young woman. Yes, he liked her personality as well as her looks. But a man had to have priorities. If he screwed up this job at KROK, his career might never recover. So he and Erica couldn't let lust get the better of them on this gig. Adam's employment history was spotty enough, and it wouldn't be fair for Erica, just starting out, to be saddled with that kind of bad mark on her record.

As their final song of the morning began playing, Erica removed her headphones and grinned at him. "How much money have we raised so far?"

He checked the note Mason had handed him earlier. "Looks like twenty-one-thousand dollars and counting. That's including Max's ten thousand."

"That's fantastic. I bet this is the biggest fund-raiser the Salvation Army has had all year. The audience must love us."

Part of him felt old and jaded next to her enthusiasm. But she definitely made this gig less of a bore. "They love you. They can hear me anytime."

"You're so sweet to say that. I was terrified I'd screw this up, like I did the last time."

He winced, remembering that fiasco. After mixing

up the ads for competing car dealers, she'd compounded the error by swearing like a sailor on air. Within minutes the phone banks had lit up with complaints from listeners, both car dealers and the FCC. Carl's face had turned purple, he'd been so enraged. He'd finally locked himself in his office and refused to talk to anyone, while Erica was sent home to contemplate her sins. Fortunately, by the next day, Carl had agreed to let her stay. "You were nervous," Adam said. "Everybody makes mistakes, especially when they're new. You just got yours all out of the way at once."

She laughed, and absently twirled a lock of her hair around one finger, a gesture he found incredibly alluring. He looked away. "I think we're supposed to tape some more promo spots this morning."

"Sure. I just want to take a break first." She was looking over the crowd, then spotted someone and waved.

Tanisha emerged from a clot of people by the door. "I brought you some goodies," she said, holding aloft a pink shopping bag.

"Great." Erica turned to Adam. "I'll be back in a few minutes."

He watched the two women head toward the rest room. Now that the initial shock of being thrown together in bed was over, maybe the next two days wouldn't be so bad. He and Erica could be friends. No reason they couldn't keep things on that level.

Carl strode over to him. "I just saw the latest donation totals. You're doing great."

"Erica's really impressed me. She has a flair for this."

"You two are great together. So far you've struck just the right tone—sexy, but not too racy. We want to tantalize, but not offend."

"I know. I've read the memos from corporate, too." To please advertisers, listeners and government regulators, stations like KROK had to dance along the edge between a little wild and too outrageous.

"Just keep that in mind. I can't step in and save your ass every time."

"I know. Like you said, I'm a man who learns from my mistakes." Had he ever learned.

Carl clapped him on the back, as close as the manager ever got to a gesture of affection, then left.

Others liked to grouse about Carl's gruff demeanor and dictatorial tendencies, but Adam owed the man too much to complain. Carl had taken a chance on him when no one else would.

Adam had been at the station less than a year when the fiasco with Bonnie happened. He'd fully expected to be back on the street, and had steeled himself for Carl's disapproval. Instead Carl had been amazingly calm. "I don't have to tell you how badly you screwed up," he'd said. "I'm taking the FCC fine out of your and Bonnie's salaries."

Adam nodded. He'd expected this.

"Since you're both involved, I can't say who's the most to blame in this, though I have my ideas," the manager continued. "But except for this, you've kept your nose clean in your time here."

He waited, wondering at Carl's choice of words.

"Your show gets good ratings. You never cause me problems with scheduling and stuff. You're never late and you don't slack off. Those things count with me, so I'm giving you another chance." Carl's eyes met his, hard as two lumps of coal. "Don't screw up again."

"I won't."

Not even Erica could make him break that promise.

"Tanisha, this outfit is definitely killer. But I don't know if I have the nerve to wear it in public." Erica stood on tiptoe and studied her reflection in the bathroom mirror. The black satin bikini panties and bra top were overlaid with a sheer black chiffon crop top and harem pants, decorated with random sprinklings of jet beads.

"Why not? Technically everything is covered except your hands, feet and belly button."

"Yeah, it has fabric over it, but I wouldn't call it covered." She did a little belly dancer shimmy. The outfit *was* flattering.

"That's the whole appeal. Covered, but uncovered. Guaranteed to drive a man wild."

She turned her back on the mirror and faced Tanisha. "Do you think Adam has a wild man in him? He's always so calm."

"Every man has a wild man inside. All that testosterone, you know."

"Right." She'd had a glimpse of that testosterone doing its stuff this morning. "If anything can bring that side of him out, this outfit should do it."

"I almost forgot. I brought you a few other things." Tanisha reached into the shopping bag and drew out a bottle of perfume and a box of condoms. "The perfume is called Seduction, and it smells divine." She handed over the bottle.

"And the condoms?"

"Better safe than sorry."

"Uh-huh." She spritzed some of the perfume on her neck. It smelled spicy, with a hint of musk. "Nice." She glanced at her watch. She had a few more minutes before she had to be back in bed. "How are things at the station?"

"Would you believe people are sending Nick get-well gifts? The mailroom is half full of everything from stuffed animals to bottles of booze. One woman even sent him a pair of her underwear."

"Ew." She made a face. "Is he supposed to wear them or sniff them?"

"I think her note said something about providing him an incentive to get well." Tanisha shook her head. "I'm just glad I wasn't the one who opened that envelope. Talk about gag!"

"Who's doing Adam's afternoon slot?"

"Audra's doing that, and they have the overnight guy in Audra's slot, and an intern from our sister station, KHOW, on overnights. Of course, Bonnie's ballistic that they didn't give her the afternoon slot."

"Why didn't they give it to her?" Erica asked. "She's qualified, isn't she?"

"They apparently offered her the overnight spot and she acted insulted."

"I don't imagine Carl took kindly to that."

"I don't think Bonnie is his favorite person, anyway."

"She can be kind of scary," Erica admitted. What had Adam ever seen in Bonnie? Besides the boobs and blond hair, of course. Erica couldn't discount the fact that men, even great guys like Adam, tended to think with their gonads, sometimes. All the more reason to turn up the heat a little by appealing to his animal instincts.

"Thanks for loaning me the outfit." She gave Tanisha a big hug.

"No problem. Let me know if it does the trick. I've got a guy I might like to try it out on."

"Oooh. Anyone I know?"

Tanisha shook her head. "He lives in my building. We've flirted in the laundry room a little."

"So maybe you'll wear this to do your laundry."

"Hey, if it works for you, I might give it a try."

A knock on the door silenced their laughter. "Erica, Carl says to get up front, pronto," Mason called.

"Be right there." She gave Tanisha another quick hug. "Wish me luck."

ADAM WAS GOING over the planned promo teasers with Mason when Erica joined them. He blinked, wondering if he was hallucinating the alarming amount of skin her new outfit displayed to an advantage. His heart pounded and he had trouble breathing. He told himself not to stare, but he couldn't keep from it. The filmy black material hid little of her from view. If anything, the fabric made the skin beneath look even creamier. More touchable...

The production assistant regained his voice first. "Erica, you look great," he said.

"Thanks." She smoothed the outfit over her hips. "I was feeling downright grungy in those old T-shirts and shorts."

"You don't look grungy now." Mason grinned.

Adam scowled at the man. Did he realize he was practically drooling?

"Thanks." She gave Mason her warmest smile. "I wanted to get into the whole spirit of this bed-in stunt. Get people talking, and contributing more money."

"You looked fine the way you were." Adam didn't mean to bark the words, but the control he'd spent all morning reclaiming was evaporating.

She moved a little closer, and lowered her voice so that he had to lean down to hear her. "Carl said to keep things sexy. What's sexier than black lingerie?"

Nothing, he thought, which immediately led to the image of her wearing just that. Nothing. *Get a grip,* he silently commanded. He cleared his throat. "He also said not to get too racy."

She looked down at the body-skimming chiffon. "This isn't too racy. People wear fewer clothes at the beach."

"We're not at the beach."

"No, we're in bed. And bed's the perfect place to wear lingerie, don't you think?"

No, he didn't think. He couldn't think. At least not rationally. They were in bed. Beds were for sleep and sex.

And he definitely wasn't feeling the least bit sleepy.

ERICA HAD COUNTED on attracting Adam's attention, maybe even making him see her in a different light. On that score, her new, more revealing outfit was definitely doing the trick. Whenever she was occupied with something else—doing an interview for the station Web site, signing autographs for people who stopped by with donations, or posing for pictures with fans—she was aware of him watching her.

Of course, as soon as she looked his way, he averted his eyes. And how funny was it that the more skin she revealed, the less he showed? He'd taken to wearing a bathrobe over his T-shirt and pajama pants, claiming he was getting a chill. As if he was fooling anyone. She knew now that he wanted her, and that knowledge was powerful.

Almost as powerful as the outfit's effect on *her*. The skimpy, slinky costume made her feel like a sex goddess. Every man who passed by her did a double-take. The thought that she could make them all hot made her feel as if she was on fire.

When everyone left for the day and at last she and Adam were alone, she was sure they'd have a chance to do something about the definite heat between them. Maybe they could cover the security lights, or hide out in the bathroom. Or something…

As soon as the front door to the showroom was locked and the lights dimmed, Adam got out of bed.

"Where are you going?" She leaned toward him, giving him a good view of cleavage. "Come back to bed."

He shook his head, and sat in one of the chairs that had been pulled up to a low table near the bed. "We need to talk, and I can't do it in bed with you. Come sit down."

Reluctantly she moved over to the chair beside him. "What did you want to talk about?" The conversation she wanted to have with him didn't require words.

He picked up a pen and jiggled it in his hand, then set it back down. "You're doing a great job," he said.

"Thanks. I'm having fun."

"That's what concerns me a little. What I wanted to discuss with you."

His words confused her. "You don't think the job should be fun?"

"It can be fun, but…" For the first time all day, he looked at her directly. "But it's serious work, too. If you don't take it seriously, you can make mistakes. Big ones."

She sat up straighter, not hiding her annoyance. "I take the job seriously."

"You haven't acted like it today."

"Excuse me, but have you checked out what we're doing here? A bed-in? It's a crazy stunt that calls for us to act a little crazy. And if you asked Carl, I bet he'd agree."

"And I'd bet he wouldn't. Not crazy in the way you've been acting. Especially in light of what happened between us last night."

She took a deep breath. Fine, if he wanted to play it that way. He wasn't the only one who could speak frankly. "It's exactly because of what happened last night that I'm doing this," she said. "I'm trying to seduce you."

To his credit, he didn't even blink. "Believe me, I know that. And it's not that I haven't been tempted…"

"Then what's the problem?" She leaned toward him, one hand on his knee. "Is it the cameras? We can cover them, or go someplace else…."

He shook his head, and gently moved her hand away. "We can't risk it. You know about the blowup I had on air with Bonnie, right?"

She frowned. "Yes. But what does that have to do with you and me…?"

"The station got a big fine over that. And another one when you had your, um, debut."

She sagged back against the chair. "I get it. You're saying if anything happens again, it could be really big trouble."

"Yes, and you're too new in your career to risk that. And I have too many other black marks against me."

"What black marks?" The Hawk was the most straight-arrow jock at the station. He never showed up so much as a minute late for work, never complained of a hangover or told the off-color jokes that were Nick's trademark. If anything, Adam had a reputation as the station intellectual. The thinking man's DJ. From what Erica could gather, the episode with Bonnie had been totally out of character for him.

"I got in trouble at a station I was at before," he said. "Big trouble. Carl was the only station manager who would even give me an interview when I came to Denver. I can't risk blowing that. Do you understand?"

She nodded. "I understand. But I think you're worrying over nothing. We aren't on air now. What we do here—as long as we stay off-camera—is our own business."

He looked at her a long moment, his eyes burning into her, searching. What did he hope to find? "It's not just about the FCC or the job," he said. "It's not a good idea for two people who work together—especially on air, in the public eye—to have any kind of relationship. There are too many complications. That's why Carl made a rule against it." He shook his head. "I don't expect you to understand, or even agree with me, but the last thing I want is more complications."

She stared at him. The man was worried getting involved with her might be *complicated?* What a complete and total cop-out. Did he think she was too much for him? Was he worried that she was another ballbuster Bonnie? Please tell her he wasn't that cliché of all clichés, a man burned by a woman and afraid to love again.

"So you don't want to start anything with me because it might interfere with our jobs," she said.

"That's right." He looked relieved. "I knew you'd understand." He stood and unfastened the tie of his robe. "It's late. Let's go to bed."

He took off the robe and folded back the covers. The thinking man's jock had obviously spent a lot of time pondering his feelings for her. Too much time.

She stood and walked around to her side of the bed. Alone under the covers, with the lights out, maybe she could find a way to turn off Adam's brain, and force him to focus on his feelings. Feelings weren't complicated at all. And she intended to do her best to see that neither of them had anything to regret come morning.

5

ERICA WAS AWARE of Adam lying still beside her. Too still. Was he holding his breath? Was he afraid he might accidentally brush against her? She turned on her side toward him. As her eyes adjusted to the dimness, she could make out his profile. "Do you think the security camera can really see anything in the dark?" she asked.

"They can see. They probably have infrared technology. You know, like nightscopes."

"What about hearing? Do you think they can hear anything?"

He didn't answer right away, as if debating his answer.

"They might."

"I don't think they do. The security guard in our building just has a bunch of television screens, showing different views. There aren't any microphones. It's probably even illegal to record customers' and employees' conversations like that."

He shifted lower under the covers. "Maybe you're right."

She slid her hand over until it brushed his thigh. The muscles contracted at her touch.

"You've got to stop," he said, his voice strained.

"Why?"

"I'm not made of stone."

She squeezed his thigh. "Obviously not." Though there was one part of him she hoped was rock-hard.

"I thought you understood why this wasn't a good idea."

"I understood why you thought so. I don't happen to agree." She scooted closer, her hand moving up his thigh, toward his crotch. He grabbed her wrist, stopping her. "You said having an on-air relationship, in the public eye, was a bad idea. But you're forgetting one thing."

"What's that?" He turned his head to look at her, his eyes dark shadows.

"We don't work together on air. Not normally. This is a special case, and it's only one more day. And two nights." She brought her other hand up to rest on his chest. "You do want me, don't you?"

"Yes." The final "S" was a hiss, like air escaping an overpressurized balloon.

"And I want you." She bent and kissed his shoulder.

"The cameras." The words came out in a croak.

She glared up at the smoked plastic bubble. "Whose idea was it to put that thing right over the bed?"

"No one asked my opinion."

"We could go somewhere else. The rest room, maybe."

"For all we know, there are cameras there, too. At least outside the stalls. Besides, what's sexy about a public toilet?"

She tried to picture them going after it in the tiny washroom and made a face. Nothing like cold tile and porcelain and the smell of commercial pine cleanser to kill the mood. She lay back on the pillow and sighed. "I hate when logic gets in the way of a perfectly good plan."

"I'm sorry. Believe me, you don't know how much." He released her hand.

"Let's just talk, then. We can do that, can't we?"

She counted three heartbeats before he answered. "Sure. What do you want to talk about?"

"You said you worked in Carmel once. Are you from California?"

"Yes."

She waited, but he didn't elaborate. "Where?" she asked. "On the coast, or in the mountains?"

"The coast. A little town called La Conchita."

"Did you surf?"

"Some."

She tried to picture a younger, tanner Adam, balanced atop a surf board. "You're a long way from the ocean for a surfer dude."

He laughed, the single sound dissolving the remaining tension between them. "Now I snowboard. What about you? Where did you grow up?"

"Right here in Denver. Can you believe it? I'm a native."

"A rare breed these days."

"So you grew up in California. How did you end up in Denver?"

He hesitated, then said. "You know how it is in this business. People move around a lot. The job brought me here."

"And how did you get to be such an expert in rock trivia?"

"My dad gave me a book about it for Christmas one year. It was something he was interested in."

"How old were you when he gave you the book?"

"Eleven. He died not too long after that." The words were matter-of-fact, but she thought she heard the pain of that long-ago loss in his voice.

"That must have been tough, losing your dad that young."

"Well, you know… Anyway, some guys memorize sports stats, with me it's always been music." The covers rustled, as if he was shrugging. "It's a way to stand out in the business."

It struck her that this was the most personal conversation they'd ever had. More so than earlier even, when he'd told her about Bonnie. Lying in bed in the dark made such intimacy seem more natural, even if they weren't touching.

She stared up at the hidden camera again. Like an unblinking eye, it could only see what was directly in front of it. In plain view. Not anything that was hidden, for instance, under the covers.

The need to touch him was overwhelming. The emotional closeness they'd found only made her crave physical closeness, too. Carefully, as if coaxing a skittish wild animal, she slid her hand across the six inches of space between them.

She heard the sharp intake of his breath when her fingers brushed his erection. He was definitely hard, and she could feel his heat through the flannel of the pajama pants. Had he been like that all day, wanting her as much as she wanted him? The thought started an insistent pulsing between her legs.

"What are you doing? You can't—"

"Why not?" She wrapped her hand around him, stroking him lightly. But that wasn't enough. She released him momentarily and moved up and slipped her hand beneath the elastic waistband.

"Erica, don't—"

He grabbed her wrist, but she shook him off and grasped his naked shaft, reveling in the satiny heat of him. "As long as we keep our movements under the covers, how will anyone on camera know what's happening?"

He lay still, letting this information sink in. "You don't think they can see our faces?"

"Turn toward me and they can't." She tugged him toward her, providing an incentive for him to do as she asked.

He rolled over onto his side, and rested his hand on her hip. "This is crazy."

"It is, isn't it?" She grinned. "Exciting too, don't you think?" She stroked him more firmly, debating diving under the covers to get her mouth around him. But anyone watching on TV would have no doubt what was going on then. Right now, they might assume the two jocks were engaging in a little pillow talk, but nothing more.

"Take your pants off," she urged. "Your shirt, too."

He hesitated, then said, "Only if you take off yours, too."

She rolled onto her back once more and wriggled farther under the covers, closing her eyes. *See, I'm just going to sleep now,* she silently told whoever might be viewing the image from the camera overhead. *All very innocent.*

The feel of the satiny sheets against her naked breasts and thighs increased her arousal. She shuddered as the fabric dragged across one sensitive nipple. When had she ever been so aware of her body, so consumed by need?

She had scarcely pushed her pants to her ankles when Adam's hand rested on her stomach, pinning her. "You're so hot," he murmured, and slid his hand farther, up to her breasts.

"I'm glad you think s—" The words dissolved into a moan as his fingers closed around one breast, massaging her, cupping her, then lightly pinching her nipple.

"I've always thought you were hot. Even if you are too young for me."

"I'm twenty-five," she said. "Not so much younger."

His hand stilled. "I thought you weren't a day over twenty-one."

"I know I'm older than most interns, but it took me a while to decide on a major in college." She'd started out in kinesiology, thinking she could be a physical education teacher. Then she'd moved to journalism, before finally settling on broadcasting. She put her hand over his, encouraging him to continue fondling her. "But I promise, I'm plenty old enough to do this."

He took the hint, and tugged hard at her nipple, then moved his hand to the other breast. "Ohhhh." She let her breath out in a slow stream.

"Don't forget the camera," he whispered, his mouth close to her ear. She forced her eyes open, and stared up at the camouflaged lens, forcing her face to remain impassive, to not reveal the desire storming through her.

He moved away from her breast and she gasped with regret, but his touch returned quickly. His fingers were wet now, playing with the nipple, sliding it between thumb and forefinger, tugging at it, rolling it against his palm.

She bit her lip to keep from crying out, and pressed her bottom against the sheet, resisting the urge to squeeze her legs together. "That feels so good," she gasped.

She was wet and throbbing, more than ready for him, but he was in no hurry to leave her breasts. He transferred his attention to the other peak, stroking and fondling until she was on the very edge of control. She closed her eyes and sucked air in through her nose, her hands clutching at the mattress.

"I wish I could see you," he said. "Naked, like this. Your nipples hard and wet from my mouth."

All she could manage in answer was a moan. How had this happened? She'd intended to be in charge here, yet now he had her helpless, every inch of her focused on his fingers roving over her and the hard knot of need between her legs.

He hooked his leg over hers and pulled it toward him, so that she lay spread-eagle beneath the covers. He trailed his fingers down her stomach, scarcely touching her, sending a flutter through her middle.

She arched toward him, craving his touch, but he didn't satisfy her immediately. He brushed his fingertips across her curls, and then his palm, then traced one finger along the top of her thigh, where it met her torso. "You're teasing me," she protested.

"Payback for what you've been doing to me all day."

She heard the smile in his voice. "It's a good thing we were sitting down most of the day. I don't think I could have walked, the condition you had me in."

"You're terribly stubborn. I had to take drastic measures." Her voice rose on the last syllable, as he plunged one finger into her. The movement startled her and sent a fresh wave of more intense arousal slicing through her. Her muscles tightened around him, trying to hold him in her as he withdrew.

"Do you like that?"

"No, I hate it. Can't you tell?" She turned her head toward him and saw him bring his finger to his mouth and suck on it. Tasting her. The intimacy of the gesture brought a knot of emotion to her throat. "I'd rather have your cock in me, but for now, your finger will do."

Her words had the desired effect. He immediately returned his hand to her crotch, his forefinger sliding into her while his thumb pressed against her clit. She moaned as a second finger joined the first, and his thumb began to brush back and forth across her clit. No more gentle teasing now. He was focused and thorough, bringing her to the very edge of her need and over.

She arched toward him, fighting against the need to moan, or even scream. The battle between the appearance of self-control and the need for release somehow intensified every sensation. Her climax pulsed through her in waves, each one deeper and more intense than the one before. A low, keening cry escaped her lips. By the time Adam brought his hand to lay between her breasts, he was trembling, as if shaken by the intensity of the moment, or his own growing desire.

She reached for him, her hand grasping his erection firmly, wanting to satisfy him the way he'd satisfied her. His fingers wrapped around her wrist, stilling her. "Wait a minute," he said. "Let me catch my breath."

They lay there for a long moment. In the stillness, she heard the ticking of a nearby clock, followed by the hum of the air conditioner as it cycled on. Then she became aware of Adam's breathing, faster at first, then a more normal rhythm. He relaxed his hold on her wrist. "All right. Go for it."

She started to comply, then smiled, remembering the way he'd teased her. She slid her hand down and grasped his balls. His body jerked, and air hissed from his lips. Taking another hint from his technique, she brought her hand up and licked the palm and fingers, then moved back to cup him. She began to stroke the underside of his shaft with one finger. A single tendon or blood vessel stood out in sharp relief, pulsing with each pass of her finger. He groaned.

"Remember the camera," she whispered. "Pretend someone's watching."

"I don't know how to tell you this, but that isn't exactly a turnoff for me."

She laughed. "Me, either. It's kind of exciting." She moved her hand up to the head of the shaft. A single drop of fluid was poised there, and she spread it across the head with the tip of her finger. "Even if we can't afford to give them a real show."

She licked her other hand and brought it alongside the first, turning toward him to get a better grasp. If she closed her eyes, would their anonymous—and possibly mythical—watcher think she'd gone to sleep?

But she opened her eyes again. She wanted to watch Adam's face when she made him come.

She encircled his shaft with both hands, fingers laced, and began to slide up and down, twisting slightly at the top before starting down again. She'd read an article once that had assured her this technique was effective and devastating, but before now she'd never had a chance to test the theory. Judging by the way Adam's eyes rolled back in his head and he clenched his teeth and arched his spine, she'd say the author of the article was on to something.

His breathing was ragged and she found herself matching him, breath for breath, her own desire spiraling upward again right along with his. There was something very erotic—incredibly intimate—about being in charge of someone else's pleasure this way. Always before, sex for her had been a matter of each partner taking what they needed from the other, each absorbed in their own satisfaction, though aware of their partner's pleasure. This moment with Adam was different, each taking turns focusing solely on the other, each allowing the other to give an incredible gift, something precious only the other could offer.

She felt the moment he was about to come, his body tensed, straining toward release. She increased the pressure of her movements slightly and, risking the camera's unrelenting gaze, she laid her head on his chest, wanting to be closer to him.

His arm wrapped around her, drawing her near, even as he came in her hand. She cupped one hand over the tip, capturing his warm, sticky essence, feeling him pulse in her palm, until he sagged back against the mattress, his arm still holding her to him. "Tell me this is not another erotic dream," he said.

"Another? Have you dreamed about me before?"

He turned his head to look at her. "Let's just say you've been the featured attraction a time or two." He groped on the floor beside the bed and came up with his T-shirt. "You can use this to clean up. I'll get another."

She wiped her hands, then retrieved her nightclothes from the foot of the bed. "I think I'll just go freshen up," she said.

"Yeah. I'll go when you're done."

When she came out of the bathroom, he was waiting for her. He'd put his pajama pants back on, but his chest was bare. Before she could speak, he pulled her to him and kissed her. It was an urgent, heated kiss, his lips pressed to hers, his tongue sweeping between her parted lips, stealing breath and sense and speech. And it ended all too soon, and he pulled away. "I don't think the cameras can see us here," he said. "But in any case, I had to do that."

He slipped into the bathroom before she could think of anything to say. She put a hand to her still-tingling lips and stared after him. For a man who'd been reluctant to get involved with her, he was certainly moving along quickly. Her theory that the thinking man had a more passionate side had proved absolutely true.

BONNIE SAT at the bar in a downtown hotspot, nursing a drink. For a Saturday night, things sure were slow. So it was raining outside. Was that any reason not to get out and have a little fun? God knew she could use a good time, since she was surrounded all day by people who were determined to bring her down.

She tapped her toe to the beat of the latest single by Nelly Furtado, but she lost her groove when the music faded and a commercial came on.

"This is the Hawk."

"And this is Erica, coming to you from Mattress Max's showroom at Wadsworth and East Six."

"We're headed toward the final day and night of our bed-in to raise money for the Salvation Army's new homeless shelter. We'll be open all day Sunday, so stop by and see us and make your donation."

"We've raised over ten thousand dollars so far, but we'd like to raise at least five thousand more in the next twenty hours."

"So come on by, folks, and help us reach our goal. We'll—"

"Turn that thing off," Bonnie snapped at the bartender.

He looked up from stacking glasses. "What?"

"The radio. Turn it off. Or at least change the channel."

He started to argue, then wisely thought better of messing with the Bombshell, and turned the dial to another station. Country and western music filled the bar. Bonnie made a face, then picked up her drink and moved to a table.

She hoped Adam and Erica were making each other miserable up there in that bed. Thank God she hadn't gotten saddled with that assignment. Imagine seventy-five hours with that turkey. She should know!

Not that Adam had been a terrible bed partner. He

had a great bod, and knew how to use it. But the man was so infuriatingly straight. He never drank more than one drink when they went out. He didn't smoke and didn't approve of her smoking. She'd made the mistake of offering him a line of coke once and he'd gone ballistic. The man ought to be a preacher instead of a rock DJ.

He was probably being a perfect gentleman with little Miss Erica. How old was she? Seventeen? Probably older than that, though she looked like a high school cheerleader. She dressed like one, too, in cute little skirts and tight little T-shirts. Like every other teeny-bopper in the mall.

Bonnie smoothed her own skintight halter dress in place. If you were a radio personality that meant you had to have personality. Pizzazz. Erica had none of that. She didn't even have a decent handle. Adam had called her "Effervescent Erica." What kind of a nickname was that? It sounded like a soda pop, or an antacid.

It wasn't like Bombshell Bonnie. That was a great name that listeners responded to. It said "Fun" and "Hot" and "Wouldn't you like to know *her?*"

She snagged a passing waitress and ordered another drink. The fans loved Bonnie. The problem was, Carl had it in for her. He obviously didn't like strong women. He'd rather give the drive-time slot to someone like Audra, who was fat and pregnant and not the least bit glamorous, than let a star like Bonnie grab the spotlight. Maybe he realized if he let her work the show for even three days, the Hawk would be history. Who wanted "the thinker" when they could have a Bombshell?

If she could find a way to get rid of Adam, Carl would have to give her the show. The trick was to come up with something that would make him look bad, while making herself look good.

It was only a matter of time before she found the right opportunity and seized it. That was one thing a bombshell always had on her side, right? The element of surprise.

6

"ALL THIS RAIN is bad for business." Carl stood at the showroom window Sunday morning, watching the weather. "Only a crazy person would be out in this mess."

"Guess that makes us crazy," Adam said.

Carl turned to him. "You look like hell. What's the matter? Not sleeping at night?"

"Um, not that great." He gulped coffee and gazed out the window, memories of last night with Erica spinning through his head. He couldn't believe he'd had some of the most amazing sex of his life, and they'd used only their hands.

He'd told himself he was absolutely not going to get involved with her, no matter how much he was tempted. He'd even been relieved when she suggested they talk. Words were safe, easy to control. He could choose them carefully, even shut them off if he felt she was probing too deeply into things that didn't concern her.

And yet, lying beneath the covers with her, darkness closing in around them, he'd found himself telling her things no one else knew. About his father. About growing up in California. How was it possible for two people to be so intimate, both physically and mentally, when they couldn't even see each other's face or lie in each other's arms?

The experience left him shaken. How long had it been since he'd felt that…that close to anyone? That alone should have made it easy to put an end to whatever they'd started.

Instead he was like an addict who'd had his first hit of a heady drug. All he could think about now was how much he wanted more. If last night could be so mindbending, what would happen when they had actual intercourse?

"Are you listening to me?"

"Huh?" He turned to find Carl frowning at him. "Sorry. I spaced it for a minute there. What did you say?"

"I said you and Erica have done a great job. I appreciate you showing her the ropes."

He shrugged. "She's great. A natural, really." His eyes drifted to where Erica, still in the black lingerie, was talking with a couple of furniture store employees, laughing, her head thrown back, her throat white and smooth above the black filmy fabric of her top. What would it be like to put his lips right there…? He shook his head. "Uh, the listeners seem to really like her."

"What about the two of you? You get along okay?"

"Yeah. Sure." More than okay. He usually took his time getting to know people, letting them reveal their true colors. After the fiasco with Bonnie, this applied double to women. But since the first day he'd met Erica he'd had trouble keeping her at arm's length. She was so easy to be with, he ended up letting down his guard.

That was asking for trouble, but he had a hard time fighting his attraction for her.

"We'll have to find a way to use her more often," Carl said.

The main showroom door burst open and a tall, wild-haired man in a loud checked suit strode into the room. The two workers who'd been talking with Erica scattered as Mattress Max himself breezed past. "Look alive, everybody!" he called. "This place is going to be filled with customers in the next hour. Let's get ready to sell some furniture."

Hand outstretched, he zeroed in on Carl and Adam. "Husack! What do you think of my promotion idea now? Am I a genius or what? Business is up sixteen percent over an average weekend. And did I read right? Over ten thousand for Sally's Army? The public loves it."

"It was a great idea," Carl said. He turned to Adam. "Have you met Adam Hawkins? He's one of the jocks participating in this fund-raiser."

Max pumped Adam's hand. "Aren't you supposed to be in bed, son?"

"Um, just taking a break." Adam set aside his coffee cup and looked at Carl. "Are we about ready to go on air?"

"Not so fast," Max protested. "I want to see the other half of the team. Where is she?"

"Erica, come over here and say hello to Max." Carl motioned Erica over.

Conversation ceased as the three men watched her approach. Why hadn't Adam noticed before how small her waist was, and how round her hips? Or was it just that the low-slung pants she wore accentuated those features? She still held a coffee cup, pink-polished nails pressed against the white foam. All he could think about was the way she'd held him last night.

"My, my, my, you certainly are a lucky dog, Mr. Hawk, or whatever your name is. Three days in bed with that."

Max's voice was low, but Adam was sure everyone around them heard the remark. He glared at the man, but the furniture store pitchman didn't even notice. He was too focused on Erica. Adam resisted the urge to elbow him in the ribs.

Carl didn't seem to notice. "Max, you remember Erica. Erica, Max wanted to say hello."

She smiled and offered her hand. "So nice to see you again." Except for the way she was dressed, she might have been at a corporate cocktail party.

"The pleasure is mine." Max kept hold of her hand and flashed a toothy grin. "Is that Therapedic 9000 comfortable enough for you?"

"Oh, yes, it's great," she said. "I wish I had one at home."

"I'm sure we could arrange a substantial discount for you." Max's grin widened, revealing pointed canine teeth.

Adam didn't want to think about what the lecher might want in exchange for a discount. He took Erica's other hand and pulled her toward the bed. "Sorry to break this up, but we need to get to work."

"Max in person isn't nearly as in your face as he is on the air," she said as she crawled into bed after him.

Adam's head throbbed with the beginnings of a

headache. "You didn't notice him ogling you? He was practically panting."

"Ogling me?" She laughed. "Adam, he's old enough to be my father."

"Since when does that stop a man?"

She reached back to fluff the pillow behind her. "You're imagining things. He's way more interested in selling mattresses than in me."

"You're kidding yourself if you think any man in this room is interested in anything besides you in that outfit."

"You think so?" Her smile hit him right between the eyes, dazing him. "That's the sweetest thing anyone's ever said to me."

He hadn't said it to be sweet. In fact, he was in a particularly sour mood at the moment, and he hated it. One night with Erica and he was behaving like a spoiled child whose toy had been admired by someone else. Erica wasn't a toy, and he had no claim on her. So why was he acting this way? He wasn't a man prone to jealousy. In fact, in the past various girlfriends had accused him of being too indifferent.

He picked up the clipboard from the bedside table and adjusted his mic as the producer gave the signal to start. "Good morning, and welcome to day three of our bed-in at Mattress Max's Furniture showroom, here at Wadsworth and East Six. If you've been hiding under a rock all weekend, or sleeping off that wild party, my partner in crime here, the lovely Erica and I, have been in this king-size bed on the showroom floor since Friday morning."

"We're raising money for the Salvation Army's new

homeless shelter in Arvada," Erica continued. "So far we've reached twelve thousand, eight hundred and six dollars. But we're greedy. We want more. Yeah, it's Sunday. It's raining. But so what? We're here, and we want you here, too. The more the merrier."

"Sounds a little kinky to me." The remark earned him another smile. "But hey, come on down. Bring by your donations and visit with all of us."

"Bombshell Bonnie will be dropping by in a few minutes with weather and traffic updates." Erica read from the clipboard.

"And we have a very special guest on the show this morning," Adam said. "Naughty Nick himself will be calling in to let us know how his recovery is going."

He cued up the music. The first chords of Stevie Ray Vaughn's "Flooding Down in Texas" filled his ears.

He pulled off the headphones and checked his watch. "Have you seen Bonnie?" he asked Erica. "She's up next."

Erica shook her head. "Maybe she's caught in traffic. I didn't know Nick was calling in. He must be doing much better."

"I hope he's not too strung-out on drugs. We don't have a thirty-second delay here like we do in the studio. No telling what he'll say."

"Let me through, people, I've got a show to do."

The crowd parted to reveal Bonnie, rain dripping from her white vinyl slicker and matching boots. Her boyfriend-du-jour, a muscular blond Adam vaguely remembered was named Doug, trailed in her wake.

"Where's my microphone?" she asked as she approached the bed. "Would somebody get me a cup of coffee? Man, it's a bitch out there."

Doug helped her off with her slicker while an assistant brought a cup of coffee and another handed her a headset. She arranged the headset, sipped her coffee, then turned to the bed. "My, don't you two look cozy." The smile she gave them was anything but sweet. Adam bit back a caustic remark.

"Hi, Bonnie," Erica said.

Bonnie ignored the greeting and gave Adam a cool look. "Let's get this over with."

The song ended and he realized he'd missed his cue. But Erica picked up the slack. "Bombshell Bonnie is here with weather and traffic. What's it like out there this morning, Bonnie?"

"Weather and traffic are all f-fouled up out there." She turned her back on the bed, playing to her audience of radio personnel, furniture store employees and early shoppers. "Wrecks working at Sims and Union, in the Eleven Hundred Block of Colfax, the I-70 and I-225 interchange, I-25 and Federal and I-25 and Santa Fe. Lights are out at Wadsworth and Alameda. Exercise caution when driving through standing water, as flooding may occur. And it doesn't look like conditions will improve anytime soon. This storm cell is expected to hover over the area into tonight. Sounds like great weather for staying home and cuddling up with a significant someone."

"Or you could come on down to Mattress Max's showroom and make a donation to our fund for the Salvation Army," Adam grabbed the segue. "While you're here, check out the full line of Therapedic mattresses."

"After all, if you're going to cuddle, why not make your love nest really cozy?" Erica said.

They cut to a commercial. "That was my line," Bonnie hissed as soon as their mics were no longer live.

"What?" Erica looked confused.

"The line about the cozy love nest. That was my line." She stabbed a finger at the script on the clipboard.

"I'm sorry, Bonnie. I didn't see the little 'B' in the margin."

"That innocent act may fool some people, but it doesn't impress me." Bonnie took a step toward Erica.

"I told you I was sorry." Erica sat up straighter and glared at Bonnie. "There's nothing I can do about it now, so get over it."

"Who are you, telling me to get over it? You just remember I'm the star here, and you're still an intern—"

"Cool it, Bonnie." Adam got out of bed and inserted himself between the two women. "Erica didn't mean anything by it."

"Come on, people, break up the coffee klatch." Carl stepped between them. "Bonnie, your segment's over. It's time for Nick's call."

Overacting the role of the wounded party, complete with tortured sighs and much hair-fluffing, Bonnie turned and left.

Carl handed Adam a cordless phone. "Nick's already on the line. We'll put him on after the next song. The production guys will patch in the call. Just ask him the usual questions—how he's feeling, if he's giving the nurses any trouble, all that."

Adam put the phone to his ear. "Hello, Nick?"

"Hey. How's it going, Adam?"

"Okay. We're going to go live in a couple of minutes. How are you doing?"

"How do you think I'm doing?" Nick's voice sounded even rougher than usual, as if he'd been smoking cigarettes and drinking shots of whiskey for three days straight. "I'm in pain, I'm bored, I'm stuck here in this bed and I can't even take a piss without help."

"Sorry to hear that."

"I'll just bet you are. While I'm dying over here, you're lolling around in bed all day and night with a gorgeous young woman. So how are you and Erica getting along? Nudge, nudge, wink, wink."

He pressed the phone tighter to his ear and glanced at Erica. She was reviewing the morning's play list, apparently oblivious to Nick's comments. "She's doing a great job," he said. "You'd never know she hadn't been doing radio for years."

"That dull, huh? Sorry. You know, anytime you like, Naughty Nick would be happy to give you a few pointers for wowing the opposite sex. It's all a matter of having primo moves and the perfect lines and you can reel them right in."

"I never did like fishing much." He heard the closing notes of "What Passes For Love." "Okay, we're going live now." He nodded to Erica and she made the introduction.

"We have a very special guest this morning, folks. Naughty Nick is calling in from Methodist Hospital, where he's recovering from a little accident Thursday night. How are you feeling, Nick?"

"Never better. I'm on some awesome drugs. Between them and the sexy nurses in this place, I'm in heaven. I may never leave. Just do my show from a bed here, with a nubile young nurse on either side of me, to fluff my pillows and tuck me in."

Adam made a face. Where did Nick come up with this stuff? "So you'd make our fund-raising bed-in a permanent thing?"

"Why not? You and Erica are enjoying it, aren't you?"

"We're having the time of our lives," Erica said. "Lolling around in bed all day, waited on hand and foot. What's not to love?"

"Yeah, but I want to know what goes on after the lights go out," Nick said. "What kind of fun are you having, then?"

"I'll never tell," Erica teased. "But I will say that the Therapedic 9000 is certainly a *comfortable* mattress. I feel great no matter what position I'm in."

"But what position is your favorite?" Nick asked. "Maybe that would be a good poll to take with your listeners. What position is *your* favorite?"

"I like to sleep on my back, personally," Adam said, trying to bring the conversation into safer territory.

"Who said anything about sleeping? Erica, did I mention sleeping?"

She laughed. "No, Nick, you did not."

"Speaking of sleep, we'd better let Nick get some rest," Adam said. "I'm sure he needs it, after the ordeal he's been through."

"All I've been doing is resting. I'm ready for a little entertainment. So come on, tell me all about the wild goings-on at Mattress Max's Furniture Gallery after the lights go out."

"Not nearly as wild as your imagination, Nick."

Adam signaled Mason to cue up the next song. "This one's just for you, buddy. Hope you're back on your feet real soon. Here's Crash Test Dummies with 'Afternoons and Coffee Spoons.'"

He pulled off his headphones and leaned back against the pillows. "Nick was in his usual fine form this morning."

Erica laughed. "The man's amazing. There he was complaining about how bad he felt and everything and the minute he was on air, he was really 'on.' His voice even changed."

"He's been in radio over fifteen years. He could probably do a show half asleep. And knowing Nick, he has."

"What about you? How long have you been doing this?"

"Almost ten years." Not counting an unfortunate three-year break he didn't like to think about.

"And how long has Bonnie been with the station?" she asked.

"Five years? I think she was with a small-market station somewhere in Texas before she came here."

"I don't think she likes me very much." She shook her head. "I can't believe she blew up like that over one missed line."

"Bonnie can be, um, *single-minded* when it comes to her job. Forget about the line. She goes out of her way to find slights."

"Maybe she should switch to decaf."

"Yeah. What's up next?"

"A representative from the Salvation Army is coming to talk about their plans for the shelter, we've got concert tickets to give away, more music, news and sports—the usual."

"Listen to you. This is all old hat already."

"I don't think broadcasting from a bed could ever be classified as 'old hat.'"

"It's not the usual way to begin a career, that's for sure."

"But it was a great way for me to get noticed. I'm still glad I'm doing it with you, though, and not Nick." Her smile turned seductive. "I'm sure I wouldn't be having nearly as much fun with him."

He tried to come up with some smart-mouthed answer, but the desire in her eyes sent all the blood rushing south of his brain and all he could do was pretend to consult his clipboard and take deep breaths. So much for his rep as Mr. Cool.

The woman was seriously messing with his head. One more night. He only had to get through one more night of this gig.

And then what? He'd still see her at the station and it wasn't as if he'd be any less attracted to her once they were both fully dressed.

The idea of mixing it up with a co-worker still made him uneasy, but maybe Erica was right. Maybe if they weren't actually working on the air together, they could pull off a relationship. She was terrific. Not a ticking bomb like Bonnie. Maybe it was time he let someone in his life again.

BY FOUR O'CLOCK that afternoon, the unrelenting rain had driven all but the dumb or desperate off the streets and into their homes and businesses. The sky outside the showroom window was as dark as night. The parking lot lights made watery circles on the asphalt, and the few people Erica could see from her seat at the end of the bed were hunched against the sheeting rain.

"Anyone know where we can get a good deal on an ark?" she asked no one in particular.

"The weather is the least of my worries right now." Carl emerged from a side room he'd commandeered as a temporary office and stood in the doorway, scowling.

His grim expression soon silenced all conversation and everyone turned to him, waiting. "I just got a call from corporate. Somebody's sister-in-law or wife or second-cousin or something objected to some of Nick's comments this morning during the call-in, and complained to one of the head honchos."

"What comment offended her?" Erica asked.

The lines on Carl's forehead deepened. "Something about what the two of you were up to after the store was closed. She said the show was promoting promiscuity."

"Promiscuity isn't something you have to promote," Adam said. "It's one of those things that sells itself."

Carl ignored him. "From what I gather, the powers-that-be weren't too upset about it. Then somebody came across a photo of Erica someone posted on a city Web site."

"A photo of me?" She raised up on her knees. "What was wrong with the photograph?"

"Apparently someone at corporate thinks the outfit you're wearing is too suggestive."

She looked down at the see-through harem pants and cropped top. Of course this getup was suggestive. That was the whole point.

"So she'll put on some different clothes and we'll keep Nick off the air until this is done," Adam said.

Carl shook his head. "They say to pull the whole thing. We've got thirteen thousand dollars for the shelter, Max has his publicity. It's time to call it quits."

"But we can't do that," Erica said. "We have to finish what we've started. Besides, if we quit now, we won't get the ten thousand Max promised."

"Have you talked to Max about this?" Adam said. "What does he say?"

"I haven't talked to him, but I know he won't like it. I can't say as I blame him. We advertised we'd be here for seventy-five hours."

"If he's upset about us quitting early, he for sure won't make the donation," Erica said.

"If he's mad enough, he might pull his ads," Adam said.

"I'll talk him out of that." Carl rubbed the back of his neck and nodded toward the bed. "You two get dressed. Everybody else, pack up."

"Carl, no." Erica jumped out of bed and ran after him. "You heard the Salvation Army captain who was here this morning. That ten thousand dollars means a lot to them."

"My job means a lot to me."

"Advertisers mean a lot, too," Adam said. "Tell corporate Mattress Max threatened to sue you for backing out of an agreement. Tell them he's one of our biggest advertisers. They wouldn't want to lose all that money, I know."

"It's advertisers they're worried about. Ones besides Mattress Max."

"Tell them we'll tone it down," Erica said. "I'll wear

something less revealing. And no more off-color remarks."

"It's only one more night and morning," Adam said. "If we quit early, it would only stir up more controversy and rumors. I'm sure corporate doesn't want that."

"All right." He frowned at Erica. "You get some clothes on. And I don't want even one little slipup from either one of you. We've got to come out of this looking good."

"We will, I promise." She ran back to the bed and grabbed up her duffel. So she wasn't thrilled about returning to her flannel pjs. And their new vigilance probably meant the chances of any more hanky-panky with Adam—at least for the rest of their stay at the furniture gallery—was out of the question.

But getting the money for the shelter was important, and so was proving she could do a good job. If she and Adam had to adopt a hands-off policy, so be it. At least they could spend the night talking. And when this gig was over, they could expand on what they'd started last night. The mattress at her apartment wasn't as deluxe as this one, but by the time they were naked again, alone, she doubted Adam would have any objections.

7

THE RAIN CONTINUED to pour into the evening. Even inside the showroom, Erica could hear the steady rumble of thunder and see the occasional flash of lightning. She was almost glad for her flannel pajamas by the time the security guard locked the front door and dimmed the showroom lights. The bad weather had put a definite chill in the air. Or maybe it was their reprimand from corporate. Despite the positive spin she'd put on the news earlier, now that she'd had a few hours to think about it, the more her anger and hurt grew.

"I can't believe they were worried about a few suggestive comments and a perfectly acceptable pair of pajamas," she said.

"That's the climate these days." Adam tucked the covers across his lap. "Advertisers are skittish. It's easy to push the envelope too far and they start pulling away."

"It just seems so unfair—getting in such a snit about such little things."

"They have to draw the line somewhere." He settled back against a stack of pillows. "And be honest. Didn't you tell me when you first heard about this stunt, you thought it was sleazy?"

She nodded. "KROK is sort of known for its sleazy stunts," she said. "But once I was here and actually part of things, it didn't seem sleazy at all. It's been fun." She reached over and touched his arm.

He looked up at the ceiling, at the smoked plastic cyclops neither one of them could completely forget. "We have to be careful."

"I know." She withdrew her hand and sat crosslegged beside him. "So let's talk."

"Isn't that what got us into trouble last night?"

"I didn't hear you complaining."

No, he hadn't complained. He'd surrendered gladly, tired of fighting his attraction for her. Learning she wasn't as young as he'd feared helped, but so did the fact that he felt more at ease with her than he had with anyone in years.

"I think I know why Bonnie was giving me such a hard time this morning," she said.

"Oh? Why is that?"

"She's jealous. She's still got a thing for you."

His breath rushed out of him and he sat up, coughing. "Bonnie hates my guts," he protested.

"She doesn't. I don't see how she could. Why bring her current boyfriend around unless she was trying to make you jealous by parading him in front of you?"

He shook his head. "No way."

"You don't think she still cares about you?"

"Bonnie cares about Bonnie. That's it. More likely she's jealous of you being in the spotlight instead of her. It's no secret she wants her own show."

"Why doesn't she have one yet?"

"Probably because Carl doesn't trust her. You heard she cussed me out on the air, right?"

She nodded. "But he gave you a second chance after that. He gave me a second chance after I flubbed those commercials."

"We're not talking one little slip of the lip," he said. "She called me a rat bastard and several other choice expletives."

He didn't seem terribly upset about the incident, at least not now. "What happened? I mean, what led to your fight, anyway?"

He was silent for a long moment. Erica flushed. "Hey, if you don't want to talk about it…"

"No, that's okay." He glanced at her. "I just hate to admit I was such a fool."

"What do you mean?"

"I should have seen what Bonnie was like right away. But I was new in town, and I hadn't been in a relationship in…a while. And let's face it—she's gorgeous and sexy and I'm a guy, so I wasn't exactly doing a lot of thinking when she came on to me." He shrugged. "It seemed like a good idea at a time. Does it bother you to hear this?"

She realized she was sitting hunched over, her hands balled into fists in her lap. She forced herself to relax against the pillow, palms flat on her thighs. "Of course not. I'm glad you're being so honest with me."

"Anyway, we only dated a couple of months. It didn't take me too long to wake up to the fact that she wasn't a very nice person."

"So you decided to break up."

"Yeah. That's when I made stupid mistake number two. Number one being ever getting involved with her in the first place. I gave her the news that I thought we should cool it right before I started my show that afternoon. By the time she came on to do the weather, she'd worked herself into a real lather. I was so stunned I didn't kill her mic nearly fast enough."

"And the FCC fined you both."

"And the station. And Carl threatened to fire us both, though eventually he calmed down."

"So if she's not still carrying a torch for you, maybe she's holding a grudge."

"I'm sure Bonnie has a long list of grudges."

"She's a very unhappy person."

"Don't waste your time feeling sorry for her."

"I'm not going to lose any sleep over her, I promise." Though she didn't anticipate a restful night. Not with Adam beside her, so close and yet forbidden.

He rearranged the pillow under his head, then settled back down. "I wonder if either one of us will get much sleep tonight."

She shifted lower under the covers, thighs squeezed together and memories teasing her. "Last night was amazing," she said.

"We can't risk anything like that tonight. Not after corporate already thinks we're on the edge of indecency."

She giggled. "If they only knew how indecent we've been."

"We ought to change the subject."

"I don't know. If we can't *do* anything, it might be fun to talk about what we might do."

"Fun? Or torture?"

"Maybe a little of both. But it would give us something to look forward to later."

"Yeah." He was silent, and she wondered if she should pursue the subject further. She didn't want to be a tease, but there was something erotic about forced abstinence. It lent a sharp edge of desire to every accidental brush of their hands or meeting of their eyes.

"So what would you do—if we were free to do anything?" His question broke the silence.

She closed her eyes and thought for a minute. "I'd start off by kissing you. Long, wet kisses, with lots of tongue. I'd want every nerve in our mouths to be aware of each other."

"I'd trace my tongue along that gap in your teeth," he said, his voice rough with emotion. "And kiss that soft spot under your chin, where your skin is so pale."

She swallowed hard, but went on, managing to keep her voice steady. "I'd kiss my way down your naked chest, until I reached your nipples. I'd tease them with my tongue, to see how sensitive they are."

He cleared his throat, and shifted under the covers. "Half a dozen times today, when I was supposed to be working, I'd catch myself staring at your breasts. At the way they curved over the top of that little bra thing under that sheer top. I'd imagine running my tongue over that curve, then dipping beneath the fabric to stroke your nipples."

Her nipples tightened at the image he painted, and she brought her own hands up to cover them, trying to squeeze out the ache.

"Are you touching yourself?" He rose on one elbow and faced her in the dark.

She stilled her hands. "Y-yes."

"That turns me on, thinking about it. I wish I could turn on the light and watch."

"I wish you could, too." What would it be like to see him, desire in his eyes, knowing he was hard, wanting her, as she brought herself to climax?

Lightning slashed the sky, followed by a low rumble of thunder. She glanced toward the showroom window, but couldn't make out anything in the darkness.

He lay back on the pillows with a groan. "I'd make love to your breasts with my mouth, kneading them, sucking and licking your nipples until you were moaning and writhing beneath me."

"Yes." She resisted the urge to reach down and find some relief. "Then…then what would you do?"

"Your turn," he said. "What would you do to me?"

"I—I'd trail my tongue down to your navel, then farther down, to your cock. I'd wrap my fingers around the shaft, and feather little kisses around the underside, maybe licking a little, feeling you pulse in my palm."

"This is crazy. Neither one of us is going to sleep tonight."

"It is crazy," she said. "But I'm not sorry I'm here with you. Even if I can't touch you."

"Me, neither."

A brilliant strobe of lightning filled the showroom with white-hot light. She squealed and dove under the covers as thunder rattled the windows. The bedside lamp went out, along with the security lighting, plunging them into sooty darkness.

She pulled the covers up to her chin and strained to hear anything over the pounding of her heart. "Adam?" she asked after a moment, her voice high and uncertain.

"I'm right here."

"Do you think it hit the building?"

"I think it might have struck the transformer. The electricity's out."

She swallowed hard. "Maybe now wouldn't be the time to mention that I'm afraid of the dark."

"There's a little light. From the Exit signs. They must be on batteries." He looked toward the red glow near the front door.

"Not enough."

"It'll be okay. Give me your hand." He reached across the covers and touched her wrist.

She clasped his hand. He had long fingers, with short nails and smooth palms. His skin was warm, his touch firm and reassuring.

"I promise I'm not going to freak or anything," she said. "I just get a little uncomfortable when I can't see anything."

"Your eyes will adjust in a minute." He scooted closer and put his other arm across her chest, just under her breasts. "Is this better?"

"Uh-huh." At least now she wasn't thinking about being afraid of the dark. She was aware of the heat of his skin against the underside of her breasts, and the hard length of his thigh next to hers. "Adam?" she whispered.

"What?" he asked, also whispering.

"If the transformer blew, that means the electricity will be out for a while, won't it?"

"Probably so. They probably have trouble all over town."

She rolled onto her side facing him, searching his

face as her eyes grew accustomed to the dim light, her heart pounding with anticipation. "So…if the electricity is out…that means the security cameras don't work."

Adam lay still, letting the idea sink in, savoring the possibilities of this unexpected turn of events. "No one's watching us."

"No one."

"So no one will see if I do this." He shaped his hand to the curve of her cheek and drew her lips to his.

He'd been preoccupied with wanting her all day, but when their mouths met his need for her blotted out all other thought. She opened her mouth and her tongue twined with his, tasting and teasing. He traced the curve of her lips, then slid along the little gap between her upper front teeth, satisfying his curiosity as to how that would feel.

She giggled, but when he would have withdrawn, she sucked hard, holding him captive.

He had no objection to prolonging the kiss, but he wanted more. Lips still locked to hers, he caressed her side, then slipped his hand beneath her T-shirt.

She sighed when he stroked the underside of her breast, and gasped when he dragged his palm across her distended nipple. "You like that?" He spoke with his lips still against hers.

"Uh-huh. Don't stop."

"I won't stop. I promise."

Her eagerness fueled his own desire, and he moved his hand to her other breast, fingers tracing the curve of the underside, thumb flicking across stiffened nipple. Listening to her gasp and moan was making him pretty stiff, too. He raised up on one elbow, and tugged the shirt to her shoulders. She took the hint and stripped the garment off over her head and sent it sailing. Her pants followed, and she lay naked beside him.

"I wish the light was better," he said, resting his palm against her stomach, feeling her skin quiver at his touch.

"You'll just have to pretend you're a blind man," she said. "And learn about me through touch."

"And taste." He took one nipple in his mouth, and swirled his tongue around and over the sensitive nub. She arched against him, her pubic bone pressed against his erection, leaving no doubt what she wanted.

He could have taken her right then, and neither one of them would have felt cheated, but he saw no reason to rush. He turned his attention to the other breast, sucking and licking, aware of her growing agitation. She writhed beneath him and made mewling sounds. "Don't stop," she whispered again. "Don't stop."

He slid his hand down, over the curve of her hip, along her muscular thigh, then dipped down between her legs, to the wet heat of her sex.

He slipped two fingers inside her, and felt her tighten around him. His erection pulsed, insistent, but he forced himself to resist the urge to bury himself inside her, now.

"That feels so good," she said, the words breathed out like a sigh.

"You haven't felt anything yet." He withdrew his fingers and brought them to her mouth. She sucked hard, and he felt the pull all the way to his groin.

Then she pushed his hand away and grabbed the elastic waistband of his pants. "These have got to come off," she said. Seconds later, the pants sailed out of the bed to land somewhere in the darkness.

Erica pressed her body against his, relishing the feel of his warm skin against hers, the tickle of his chest hair against her breasts, the jut of his hipbones against hers, the insistent pressure of his cock against her thigh. In the darkness every touch was intensified, every sound magnified. When she rested her head on his chest, his heartbeat was a steady pounding, a counterpart to her own erratic pulse.

She raised up on her elbows and bent her head to suckle his nipple, his breathing growing more harsh and uneven as she reached down to stroke his erection.

Remembering her earlier promise, she kissed her way down his body, pausing at his navel to trace the slight depression, rewarded by the catch of his breath.

She moved down farther. He flinched as her fingers wrapped around him, then let out his breath in a sound-less rush. She slowly dragged her hand up the length of him, marveling. "Have you been hard like this all day?" she asked.

"No." He reached down and grasped her arms and pulled her up until her face was even with his once more. "For the past three days. You've had me in agony."

"Then I promise, it will have been worth the wait."

They kissed again, a slow, drowning kiss that belied the urgency of their need. "I don't want to wait much longer," he said. "We don't know when the power will come back on."

"I don't want to wait, either." Thank goodness for Tanisha's condoms. She rolled over and dug in her bag for the box.

"What are you doing?" He snuggled against her, one hand caressing her breast, the other stroking her bottom.

"G-getting this." She held up the foil packet, breathless from the way he was rolling her nipple between his thumb and forefinger.

He took the condom. "I don't know whether to be surprised or pleased that you've been planning this."

"Why should you be surprised?" She rolled onto her back and listened to him tear open the condom packet.

"You look so young and innocent."

"I'm not innocent, and I've wanted to make love to you from practically the first time we met."

The idea intrigued him. She didn't strike him as the type of woman who went after anything in pants. What about him had drawn her? "Why me? You didn't even know me."

"You were…different. Sort of…aloof."

"And you liked that?" That didn't sound right.

"Only that you were a little mysterious." She traced a finger down his chest. "That was sexy. And you have a sexy body. And…I don't know. There was just something about you that made me want to know you better. But I was beginning to think it would never happen. You treated me like a little sister."

"I don't have a sister." He sheathed himself, then nudged her legs apart so he could kneel between them. "And if I did, I promise I wouldn't treat her anything like I've treated you."

She started to answer back, but he reached down and parted her folds, zeroing in on the sensitive nub of her clit, and words failed her. He plucked and tugged at her, insistently, then more gently. She rolled her head back and was dimly aware of an animal moan escaping her lips.

Adam plunged into her at the moment of her climax. She contracted around him, drawing him deeper, and arched to meet him, riding the waves of release that rolled through her.

As her own urgency subsided, she brought her legs up and wrapped them around him. She held him tightly, making him work for each thrust, drawing him deeply within her, until every inch of him was sheathed in her wet satin heat. She reached one hand down to cup his balls, raking the tips of her nails across the sensitive flesh.

He thrust harder, deeper, grunting with the effort, then let out a strangled cry as he came.

He rose up on his knees and cradled her bottom in his hands, so that she was more or less sitting in his lap. She sensed more than saw his smile, and realized she wore a similar expression. "That was fantastic," she said, and kissed his cheek. "Even better than I'd imagined."

"Someday I'll have to ask what you imagined, but not now." He eased out and away from her, and she scooted back against the pillows.

He got up and headed for the bathroom. She listened to his receding footsteps and thought about that word *someday*. Did that mean he saw a future for them? She sensed he was still skittish, because they worked together and maybe because of his past experience with Bonnie. But no one at the station had to know they were a couple now. It might even be fun, sneaking around behind everyone's backs.

Adam needed a little fun in his life. The man was way too serious, at least when he wasn't on the air. Maybe he was lonely. In any case, she was here now, and she was sure she had the cure for whatever ailed him.

8

THEY WOKE MONDAY morning to find the power restored and the Furniture Gallery already coming to life. There was no time for private conversation, as the morning's schedule was filled with their regular show, plus the final tally of funds raised.

Including the ten thousand dollars pledged by Max, the KROK bed-in had netted thirty-one thousand dollars for the Salvation Army.

"Best promo we ever did," Max declared when the broadcast shifted back to the station and everyone began packing to leave the Furniture Gallery. "Great for the shelter, great for my image and great for business. We sold ninety-seven mattress sets during the past three days." He beamed at Erica. "We should make it an annual event."

"You make something an annual event, you lessen the impact," Carl said. "You have to keep coming up with new things to capture the public's interest."

"You put a pretty girl in a bed—what man's not going to be interested in that? And for the women, you put a guy in there, too. Instant sex appeal."

"We'll talk about it next year." Carl put his hand on Erica's shoulder and steered her toward the door. "We've got to get back to the station."

In the parking lot, they stopped by the KROK van Carl was driving. "You two have the rest of the day off, so go home and get cleaned up or rest, or whatever you have to do," the manager said. "You did a good job."

"Thanks, Carl." She gave him a weary smile.

"I want a steak," Adam said. "No more pizza and burgers."

"Whatever. I want to see you both in my office first thing tomorrow morning." He climbed into the van and drove away.

Erica looked at Adam. "Why does he want to see us in his office? Do you think he knows what happened between us?"

"How could he? *We* could hardly see each other. There's no way anyone else saw us."

True, the showroom had been very dark. But that hadn't interfered with their sense of touch. Her nipples hardened at the memory.

"He probably just wants to give us some kind of formal thanks," Adam added.

"Or he's got some other promotion in mind." She made a face. "This turned out not to be so bad, but what if he wants us to do something really stupid?"

"We'll tell him to give the gig to Bonnie." He patted her shoulder. "Come on, let's get out of here." He stifled a yawn. "I think after my shower and my steak, I'll take a nap. For some reason, I didn't get much sleep last night."

"Must have been the storm." She stretched her arms over her head. "All that thunder and lightning kept me awake, too."

"Thunder and lightning?" His eyes met hers, his expression suggestive.

"Yep. It was pretty spectacular."

"It was, wasn't it?" He patted her shoulder, then let his hand drop. "We'll talk later."

She nodded. "Good idea." Though part of her wanted to go home with Adam right now, the rest of her realized a shower and a nap would make for a better time with him later. She started toward her car, then looked over her shoulder at him. "Hey, Adam."

"Yeah?"

"We won't be doing that much talking next time we get together. You'd better rest up. You're going to need your energy."

The interest that flashed into his eyes was worth the mad dash she had to make to her car. He stopped chasing her halfway across the parking lot and waved her on.

When she looked back, she saw Mason and another production worker surround him, laughing. She smiled and steered the car toward the exit from the parking lot. Carrying on a love affair with Adam amidst a bunch of nosy co-workers was going to be interesting. But then, she'd never been one to run from a challenge. Especially when the prize was so worthwhile.

TUESDAY MORNING, Adam arrived at work early. He told himself it was because he was eager to get back into the rhythm of a normal workday, but he knew the chance to see Erica before most of the other employees showed up had factored into his early arrival.

But she didn't appear until five after eight. By then, Adam was already in Carl's office while Audra took the morning show helm. He'd take his normal afternoon slot and Audra would do mornings until Nick was well.

"How's Nick?" Adam asked, helping himself to a soda from the mini refrigerator by Carl's desk. "When's he going to be able to come back to work?"

"Next week, maybe. They're supposed to kick him out of the hospital tomorrow."

"He's probably driving them all crazy." He sank onto the sofa. "What did you want to see me about?"

"Let's wait until Erica gets here." Carl shuffled papers, then looked at Adam again. "Now that you've had a little time to think, what's your assessment of her?"

Adam blinked, surprised at the question. *She's the sexiest, smartest, most amazing woman I've met in years.* But that probably wasn't the answer Carl was looking for. "Like I said before, she's a natural on the air. Quick thinker. Calm. She has a great rapport with the listeners."

Carl nodded. "I wanted to make sure your opinion hadn't changed. So she acted like a pro?"

"Sure. She didn't falter once."

"Good."

"Hi, Carl. Adam." At that moment, the woman herself breezed in. "Sorry I'm late. I overslept." She settled next to Adam on the sofa and crossed her legs. She'd taken the pink out of her hair and today wore it in a curly style. She looked great, as usual. "Can you imagine? All that time in bed, you'd think I'd have caught up on my sleep."

Adam bit the inside of his cheek to keep from giving away the truth about how little sleep either of them had gotten in that bed.

"Adam and I were just talking about the great job you both did with the promo," Carl said. "We got terrific listener response. Well, except for that one complaint, but that didn't harm us any."

"I thought it went really well." She smiled at Adam. "It helped having Adam there to help me."

"The two of you make a great team. I want to keep that momentum going, keep you two on the air together."

"Please don't tell me you've got another crazy promotional stunt in mind," Adam said.

"Those crazy promotional stunts keep us in business. But no, I have something bigger in mind. I want you two to do the afternoon drive-time slot together from now on."

Adam couldn't believe what he was hearing. Talk about a bad idea. If he and Erica were partners on air, no way could they team up after hours. The potential for trouble was too huge. "Carl, I don't think—"

"That's a fantastic idea!" Erica clapped her hands together, the smile on her face bright enough to light the building. "Thank you. Thank you."

About that time, Adam's objection apparently registered. She turned to him, her smile gone. "You don't want to work with me?"

"It's not that I don't think you're great," he hastened to add. "It's just that I've always done my own thing." *And I'd rather have you as my girlfriend than my working partner.*

"So the Hawk won't be flying solo anymore," Carl said. He sat back in his chair, hands folded on his stomach. "We'll call it the Hawk and Honey show."

"Honey?" Erica laughed. "I don't know if I can say that with a straight face."

"It's all in how you sell it. You're a pro, I'm sure you can do it."

"It's sexist," Adam said.

"Not sexist, *sexy*." Carl's eyebrows drew together in a V. "Is there some reason you and Erica shouldn't work together? Something you aren't telling me?"

He glanced at her. She was sitting on the edge of her seat, an eager look in her eyes. For someone like her, a prime radio slot on the biggest rock station in the market was a dream come true. No way could he ruin that dream for the sake of his own libido.

"You're right, Carl. It'll be great. The listeners are probably getting tired of me by myself anyway."

"Thank you, thank you. I promise it'll be great." She beamed at both of them. "When do we start?"

"How about this afternoon? Play up the idea that you two had so much fun together at the bed-in you couldn't bear to break up the party."

"We don't want to give people the wrong idea," Adam said.

Carl laughed. "The entertainment business is all about giving people the wrong idea. Remember, sex appeal and excitement sell. So flirt, banter, whatever works."

"That should be simple enough." She gave him a knowing look.

He shifted his gaze away from her. For Erica, it probably did seem simple. She couldn't see the problems he did, didn't know how hard it was at times to live life in the public eye. He didn't relish being the one to wake her up to reality.

WHEN ERICA LEFT Carl's office, she could hardly contain her excitement. She ran downstairs and straight to

Tanisha's desk. "Whoa, what's gotten into you?" Tanisha looked up from a stack of reports she was collating. "You look ready to float up to the ceiling."

"I feel like I could." She sank into the chair next to the desk. "The most amazing thing just happened."

Tanisha set aside the reports. "You got picked for the next season of *Survivor*? A long-lost uncle left you a million dollars? Wait—I know. Carl just doubled your salary. Now *that* would be amazing."

She laughed. "None of that, but something almost as good. Carl liked the way Adam and I interacted during the promo so much that he's putting me on the afternoon drive-time show with him!"

Tanisha's eyes widened. "You mean like a partner?"

She nodded. "Yes. Can you believe it?" The thought of working with Adam every day was too sweet. "It's incredible."

"Wow. Congratulations." She leaned forward and lowered her voice. "So you never did give me the scoop. What happened after I loaned you the lingerie? Exactly how much did you and the Hawk interact?"

Erica grinned. "Let's just say I think you should definitely try that outfit on that guy in your building. The results for me were…impressive."

"Uh-huh. Did you make use of those condoms I sent along?"

"Oh *yes*."

"Get out of here!" Tanisha slapped Erica's arm. "How did you manage that with the security cameras and everything?"

Erica looked around to make sure no one was listening, then leaned closer, keeping her voice low. "You remember that big storm Sunday night? When the power went out?"

"Yeah."

"Well…no electricity, no cameras."

Tanisha laughed. "You go. So what are you going to do now that you'll be working together on air?"

She straightened and smoothed her skirt over her thighs. "We haven't really talked about it."

"The man doesn't talk much, I've noticed."

"He's better when we're alone. I definitely want to see more of him. And I think he feels that way, too." Some men were harder to read than others. Adam had definitely been into her Sunday night, but this morning he'd seemed less sure. Maybe he was just gun-shy, remembering what had happened with Bonnie. Or maybe some other woman had screwed him up in the past. No matter. If he was reluctant, she was sure she could persuade him. After all, they still had a lot of discovering to do, both in and out of bed.

"If Carl finds out, he'll have a conniption. Probably fire you both. You, for sure, since you don't have any seniority."

"I know." She ought to be worried about that, but the idea of having to sneak around with Adam to keep anyone from finding out about their relationship made things that much more exciting. "We'll be careful."

"So you get the man, and your own show." Tanisha shook her head. "The stars are sure lining up for you. But you've still got another problem."

"What's that?"

"The Bombshell is going to explode when she hears this one."

Bonnie. For a moment Erica had forgotten about her unpredictable co-worker. "No, I don't imagine she'll be too happy."

"Are you kidding? If I were you, I'd steer clear of her for the next few days, at least."

"That's going to be hard to do, since she does the weather and traffic reports during the show."

"Yeah, well at least Adam will be there to run interference."

"I'm sure he's thrilled with that idea." Maybe that explained why he'd been less than enthusiastic about them working together.

"What are they going to call the show, anyway?" Tanisha asked. "It can't be Afternoons with the Hawk anymore."

"Carl wants to call it the Hawk and Honey show." She made a face. "Can you believe it?"

Tanisha laughed. "Honey? Sounds like something Carl would come up with. I suppose it could be worse."

"It doesn't matter." She stood, ready to get to work. "If I have to change my name to Lambchop to do this, I will."

The phone rang. "I'd better answer that," Tanisha said. "But congratulations. I can't wait to hear you on the air."

"Thanks." She turned and headed for the break room. Tonight she might treat herself to a bottle of champagne to celebrate, but for now a cup of strong coffee would have to do.

She wasn't too surprised to find Adam already in the break room, seated at one of the tables. "I thought you might come down here after you got finished with

Carl," she said as she poured the last cup of coffee from the carafe. "Did he say anything else interesting after I left?"

"No, he just wanted me to take over some of Nick's in-stores and concert gigs until he's on his feet again."

She took the seat across from him and busied herself adding packets of creamer and sugar to her coffee, while she studied him through lowered lashes. He looked more rested than he had over the weekend, the tiredness gone from his eyes. But he was never what she would call relaxed. He always had a watchfulness about him, as if he were sizing up every situation, never accepting anything at face value. No wonder he'd been dubbed "the thinker" by some since-departed station wag and that the label had stuck. But Erica wondered if it didn't mean he tended to overthink some situations.

Not that she could be accused of overthinking. If anything, she was too impulsive at times. For instance, she'd once decided on a whim to drive to California for the weekend, ditching her job and the guy she was dating without a second thought. Looking back, she could see it wasn't the smartest move, though it had been fun at the time.

But she was serious about this job, and about working things out with Adam. So rather than blow off what was bound to be an uncomfortable conversation, she faced up to the fact that they needed to talk about what had happened in Carl's office. "I know you're not too keen on giving up your solo spot in the afternoon," she said. "But I think we'll have fun together."

"I'm sure we will." He looked up from contemplating his coffee. "Hey, I didn't mean to come off negative there at first. This is a terrific opportunity for you and I know you'll do a great job. And I meant what I said about the listeners being ready for a change. They love you."

"Then what's the problem?"

He sat forward, both hands wrapped around his coffee cup. "You remember what we talked about, Sunday night? About how two people who work together shouldn't get involved in a personal relationship?"

So that was what was bugging him. She took a sip of coffee, stalling, and made a face. Urk, it tasted like dirty dishwater. She should know better than to get the last cup. "I remember. But you don't have to worry about that now."

"I don't?" He frowned. "Why not?"

"Because we've already proved that being involved with each other off the air makes it that much easier to work together."

"It does?"

"Sure. Do you think that 'sexy banter' that Carl, and the listeners, like so much would have come naturally if we weren't attracted to each other? It's because we're involved that we work so well together."

"I can guarantee Carl's not going to buy that explanation. If he finds out the two of us are seeing each other outside of work, we're both history."

Her stomach fluttered. "He won't find out. We'll be careful."

He looked unconvinced. "But what happens if things go bad between us? That means the show goes bad, too. Then we're both worse off than we were before, both professionally and personally."

"Why are you assuming things won't work out?"

"I'm being realistic. Most relationships do end at some point. What happens then?"

"I say we worry about that then." Why borrow trouble by thinking negatively now? "We're both adults. We can handle it."

"I thought I could handle Bonnie and it almost cost me my job."

She debated dousing him with her coffee, but told herself that wouldn't exactly prove her point. "That's not fair. I'm nothing like Bonnie."

He sat up straighter. "You're right. I'm sorry. But I've always tried to keep my personal life separate from my work. Every time I've deviated from that, I've ended up paying a big price."

"I don't see how we're going to do that if we're working together every day."

He looked pained. "I'm saying we need to quit while we're ahead. What happened at the Furniture Gallery was great. I'll never forget it. But we need to put it behind us now and focus on work."

She couldn't believe she was hearing him right. "You're serious? You don't want to sleep with me again? Ever?"

"Keep your voice down." He glanced around the still-empty room, then turned to her again, his voice softer. "It's not that I don't want to. But I think it would be best for both of us if we were friends and co-workers, not lovers."

He made it sound so simple. Like turning the dial to another channel. "I don't know whether to feel hurt that you could drop me so easily, or amazed at the way your mind works," she said.

"Don't be hurt. And don't think this is easy for me. But it's for the best. You'll see." He stood. "I have to go get ready for the show. Are you coming?"

"Sure. In a minute." As soon as she had time to calm down. Right now, all she wanted to do was knock some sense into him.

After he left, she got up and poured her too-bitter coffee down the sink. So Adam thought they should put what happened this weekend behind them. Go on as if it never happened.

How was she supposed to pretend the most amazing sex of her life hadn't happened? How could she treat Adam as a mere *friend and co-worker* when he meant so much more to her now?

At least he hadn't suggested she turn down the job. He must have known how much this chance meant to her. But dammit, why should she have to ignore her feelings for Adam in order to succeed in her career?

There had to be a way to have her dream job and her dream man at the same time. Surely she was smart enough to find that way.

BY THE TIME Bonnie got home that night, she had worked herself into a fury over her latest mistreatment at the hands of KROK management. Doug was waiting for her, lounging on the sofa and watching TV as if nothing in the world was wrong.

"Shut off that noise. I don't want to hear it," she snapped, and tossed her purse on the coffee table in front of him, narrowly missing an open can of beer.

He hit the off button on the remote and rescued the beer. "Tough day?"

"It was a horrible day. The worst." She whirled to face him, hands on her hips. "You'll never guess what they've done now. Never in a million years."

He sipped the beer. "So tell me."

"They've put that, that, *nobody,* Erica whatever-the-hell-her-name-is, in the drive-time slot with Adam Hawkins."

"I see," he said, looking puzzled. "And that's bad because?"

"Because I should have had that position, not some amateur like her." She began to pace, high heels making sharp round circles in the thick pile of the carpet. "Nobody even had the courtesy to warn me. I showed up to do the traffic report at four and there she was, sitting in my chair. The one I always sit in to do my reports. I couldn't believe it."

Erica hadn't even been smart enough to move out of the way. Bonnie should have known then something was up. "You'll have to stand today," Adam told her, not even bothering to apologize. "We'll try to have another chair for you tomorrow."

"What is *she* doing here?" Bonnie couldn't even look at Erica, instead focusing on Adam.

"Adam and I are doing the afternoon show together now," Erica said, as calmly as if she was announcing the time.

"Oh, are you?" Bonnie practically purred. She knew better than to let them see how she was really feeling. How *enraged* the news made her. She even smiled at Adam. "Did you suggest her for the position?" she asked.

"It was Carl's idea." Erica butted in again. "He thought listeners were ready for a change."

"If the listeners want a change, Carl should give them me," Bonnie said now to Doug. "Carl obviously hates me. He discounts all my hard work and gives some…some child, a complete amateur, her own show when she's only worked on the air a few hours."

"If he's so against you, maybe you should get a job somewhere else." Doug helped himself to an apple from the bowl on the coffee table.

"I don't want to go anywhere else. KROK is the number one station in Denver. Going somewhere else would be like taking a demotion."

Doug took a bite from the apple. "Maybe you could sue."

"Believe me, I've thought of that. But why should I have to pay a lawyer to get what I deserve?" She began to pace again. "No, I need a way to open Carl's eyes to my value at the station."

"How are you going to do that?"

"I don't know. But I'm always thinking. Always looking for my opening. And when I find it, they'll all be sorry they took me for granted."

"I don't see how anybody could take you for granted, baby."

Doug always said the right thing, one of the reasons she liked having him around. But words weren't always enough. She wanted proof that she was valued. She wanted her own radio show and the fans she deserved.

She was tired of people standing in the way of her dreams. If she had to shove them over to get what she wanted, then it was time to start shoving.

9

"THAT WAS 'Into the Morning' by The Weekend." Adam segued into the next promo. "Speaking of the weekend, on Saturday from one to four I'll have the KROK swag van at Highlands Audio, 42nd and Federal. Stop by and get your free KROK bumper stickers or T-shirts. I'll also have some CDs and concert tics to give away. While you're there, check out the great deals on home and car stereo systems."

"Would that be the brand-new swag van?" Erica asked, right on cue.

"That's the one. A replacement for the one totaled in Naughty Nick's accident. Stop by and check out the sick paint job on this baby. So what are your plans for the weekend, Erica?"

"I'll be at the Green Day concert Saturday night. And Saturday afternoon, I'm having a new bed delivered."

That certainly wasn't in the script, but he played along. "A new bed? Something you bought to celebrate our new show?"

"Not exactly. Mattress Max was so pleased with the job we did raising money for the Salvation Army that he's sending me my very own Therapedic Sleep System."

And what exactly did Max expect in return? The lecher. Adam pushed the thought away and kept up the patter. "How about that, folks? Max didn't send me a mattress. Maybe if I had long blond hair and big b—"

"Now, Hawk, you're going to give people the wrong impression."

"I was going to say big blue eyes." His eyes met hers, and his heart beat a little faster. Seeing her every day this way hadn't done anything to make him stop wanting her. Working together in the small sound booth, it was impossible not to brush up against each other a dozen times a day. And now she was talking about mattresses, reminding him of the time they'd spent alone, in the dark, in a certain king-size bed…

While he segued into the commercial break, she scribbled a note and passed it to him. *Since you didn't get a new mattress of your own, you'll just have to come over and try out mine.*

He cleared his throat, determined to steer the conversation back to safer territory. *You know why that wouldn't be a good idea,* he wrote back.

Oh, I think it would be a very good idea. She winked as she passed back the scrap of paper. He checked the countdown clock and saw it was time to go live once more.

"Good news, folks. Naughty Nick will be back on the air Monday morning. His leg's still in a cast, but he hasn't let that slow him down."

"I heard they kicked him out of the hospital for chasing nurses," Erica said.

"I heard they booted him because he *caught* one."

"I'm sure he'll have some wild stories to tell," Erica

said. "So be sure to tune in Monday morning at 6:00 a.m. for the return of Naughty Nick."

"Looks like it's time for us to say goodbye. Have a safe weekend. Casey is up next to take you out on the town for your Friday night." He hit Play and the strains of Korn's "Did My Time" blasted from the speakers.

Erica removed her headphones and grinned at him. "Our first week done. I thought it went pretty well."

"You did great." He stowed his headset and stood and stretched. He lowered his voice and moved close enough that any listening production crew wouldn't be able to overhear. "What's with the stuff about the bed?"

"It's true. I am getting a new bed this weekend." She gave him a coy look. "And you're welcome to try it out anytime."

"I am not getting back in your bed." He had to force the words out, but he meant them.

"You say that, but I know you want to be there. And I want you there."

Her words sent heat curling through him. "Enough. I told you why that's a bad idea. Nothing's changed about our situation to make it a good one."

"You're too young to worry so much." She retrieved her purse from under the console and slung it over her shoulder. "Want to go for a drink? Celebrate our first week together?"

He shook his head. "Give it a rest."

"You know what I think?"

He groaned. "No, but you're going to tell me, aren't you?"

"I think you're a masochist. You like to punish yourself. Either that, or you're afraid to have a good time."

"Thank you, Dr. Laura." He fished his car keys from his pocket and headed toward the door. "See you on Monday."

He hurried across the parking lot, hoping she'd have the sense not to follow him. So she thought it was cowardly not to follow through on his feelings for her. From his point of view, avoiding her took more guts than he'd known he had. If he'd been the type to believe in karma, he'd have said he was paying for past sins by having to struggle so hard to do the right thing now.

He was unlocking his car, almost home free, when Bonnie cornered him. "Going to meet your little girlfriend?" She leaned against the driver's side door, preventing him from opening it.

"If you're talking about Erica, she's not my girlfriend."

"Doesn't look that way to me. You two sound pretty cozy on the air."

"It's part of the act." A lie, but she didn't have to know that. Carl *had* encouraged them to flirt on air.

"You're a terrible actor. I should know. If Carl finds out you two are a hot item, he'll fire you both."

"There's nothing for him to find out. There's nothing going on between us."

He pushed her aside, and slid into the driver's seat and slammed the door. She tapped on the glass and he reluctantly rolled down the window.

She leaned down farther, and looked him in the eye. "She's only using you, you know. She's ambitious, and she saw you as a way to get what she wanted."

"Like you did, Bonnie?" He turned the key in the ignition and the engine roared to life. "Only it didn't work for you, did it?" Without waiting for an answer, he pulled away. She stumbled back from the car. When he looked in the rearview mirror, he could see her still standing there, staring after him, no doubt with hate in her eyes.

Would Erica one day look at him that way, too? As much as he told himself he wanted to put some distance between them, her admiration was a salve to his ego. One he didn't know if he could bear to give up.

HAVING STRUCK OUT with Adam, Erica talked Tanisha into going out with her to dinner. After Thai food in LoDo, they headed out to Spinnaker, a hot new dance club. "If nothing else, maybe we can meet some hot guys and dance," Tanisha said as they settled at a table.

Erica looked around at the neon-accented bar and the sunken oval dance floor. "Yeah."

"You don't sound that enthusiastic. Let me guess. There's only one guy you want to dance with right now."

"What am I going to do? As long as we're on the air he'll talk to me, even flirt with me. But as soon as that red light goes out, he can't get away from me fast enough."

"Maybe he's being smart. He doesn't want to get fired."

"It's a stupid rule."

"Yeah, but it's still a rule. Is any guy worth losing a great job?" A waitress arrived with their drinks and Tanisha handed her a ten. "I'll get this round."

"Thanks." Erica sipped her margarita. Tart and strong. Enough of these and maybe she'd work up the nerve to do something about Adam. "I've thought of trying to make him jealous, but who with? There aren't that many guys to choose from."

"There's Nick."

Both women made a face. "There's Jazzman Jerry," Erica said. "But he's, what, fifty? And he's married."

"I'm pretty sure the new intern, Davie, is dating someone. I'm pretty sure Mason is gay. And Charlie is engaged to that jock from KGSY."

Erica took another sip of margarita. "I've thought about going over to his house and demanding he have sex with me."

Tanisha shook her head. "Girl, you are pathetic. Have you thought about just playing by his rules?"

"What do you mean?"

"Accept that it's not going to happen between you two and move on. I mean, no sense mooning after some dude who doesn't even appreciate you."

Erica shook her head. "I can't do that."

"Why not?"

She looked out over the dance floor, above the gyrating mass of bodies, and debated whether or not to say out loud something she'd scarcely admitted to herself. "I just feel really…I don't know, *obsessed* with him."

"Come again?" Tanisha leaned over the table toward her, one hand to her ear. "Obsessed?"

"I know it's crazy. I don't even understand it myself. I get that way about things sometimes." About men, about jobs or even her hair. Erica would be going along with her life just fine, then out of the blue some new urge would hit her. Following those urges had led her to change majors and give up on relationships, not to mention cycle through a dozen different hairstyles, drawn by the lure of something she was sure was better.

True, such impulsive choices had often given her grief, but she knew from experience she wouldn't be satisfied until she gave into them. It was a quirk of her personality she'd learned to live with.

Besides, Adam was different. Her feelings for him went beyond mere preoccupation. She pushed aside her half-finished drink and put her elbows on the table, chin in hand. "What happened that weekend at the Furniture Gallery was amazing. We were so close."

"You ought to know by now that when a guy has sex with you it doesn't always mean anything. You were there, you were naked, you had fun—but that's not love."

"This was *different*." She shook her head. "I can't explain, but Adam and I really had a connection. We talked about all kinds of things. Just being with him felt so…so intimate. I've never experienced anything like that." In a way, it was scary, but people should confront their fears, right?

Tanisha frowned. "So you're saying the only time the man can open up is when he's having sex."

Erica straightened and reached for her drink. "I guess that's it."

"Then he has problems maybe you can't solve."

"Maybe he has problems he needs me to solve."

Tanisha rolled her eyes. "I never pegged you as one of those women."

"What do you mean?"

"Women who are attracted to men who *need* them."

"I'm not attracted to Adam because he needs me." Erica trailed her thumb around the rim of her glass. "Well, not much. I'm attracted to him because he's… he's Adam." Sweet, sexy, strong in a way she couldn't describe. She'd glimpsed a side of him most people didn't see.

"It's okay." Tanisha patted her hand. "Nobody ever said these things made sense."

Erica drained the last of her drink. "This is too depressing. Let's not talk about it anymore. What about you? How's it going with that guy in your building?"

"I saw him in the laundry room last week."

"And? Were you wearing the harem girl outfit?"

"Nah. I didn't have the guts to do that. But we talked for a while. Flirted some. I think there's a chance he'll ask me out soon."

"Why wait for him? You should ask him out."

"Maybe. I'm not sure I have the guts you do. I sure as hell couldn't seduce a man I hardly knew just because he turned me on."

"Why not? Especially if you were spending the weekend in bed with him anyway."

Tanisha laughed. "There is that." She picked up her drink, but froze with her glass halfway to her lips, her eyes widening. "Get a load of the couple that just walked in."

Erica looked over her shoulder. "Who?"

Tanisha swatted her hand. "I told you not to look. It's that redhead and her boy toy, in the S & M getup."

Erica ducked her head and pretended to dig through her purse. Out of the corner of her eye she watched a tall woman with flame-colored hair saunter across the room. As far as she could tell, *everyone* in the place was watching her. Judging by her outfit, that was exactly what Red had in mind. The black vinyl bustier and micromini hugged every curve, leaving little to the imagination. She wore stiletto thigh-high boots and her hair was drawn back in a severe ponytail. A muscular man with a shaved head trailed behind her, dressed in black leather pants and vest, a studded dog collar around his throat.

"What are they supposed to be, some kind of circus act?" Tanisha whispered.

From their table, the two friends had a good view of the dance floor and the bar. Usher began to play and the redhead led her escort onto the dance floor. Despite the other dancers crowding around them, the couple was easy to spot. The man was several inches taller than most of the men, and the woman's bright hair glowed like a candle flame even in the muted lighting of the dance floor.

"He's not much of a dancer, is he?" Tanisha said.

"I don't think she minds." The man stood in the middle of the dance floor, shuffling his feet slightly while the woman moved around him like a pole dancer. She shimmied and slid up and down him, her hands flat against his chest or clutching his shoulders. At one point she straddled his thigh and blatantly rubbed against him, their eyes locked.

Tanisha fished the olive from her martini and popped it into her mouth. "The woman is sick."

"She's an exhibitionist," Erica said. "She likes to be the center of attention."

The song ended and the pair moved off the dance

floor to the bar. The woman spoke to the bartender and in a moment he brought two shot glasses.

Her partner picked up one of the shot glasses. Red left the second glass untouched, and leaned back against the bar. But instead of drinking the shot, the man held it over her, tipping the glass until a thin stream of liquor dripped onto her throat, and ran down to the valley between her breasts.

"Is he going to do what I think he's going to do?" Tanisha asked.

"He's doing it." Erica held her breath as the man bent and ran his tongue down Red's chest, licking up the shot. Her heart pounded as she saw, not this stranger, but Adam. And *she* was the one laid back against the bar, *his* tongue cleaning up every drop of the sticky liquor.

"I can't believe they're doing that in public," Tanisha said.

"Have you ever done anything like that before?" Erica asked.

"Body shots? Not in public. That's just sick."

"Not in public. But what about in private?" She turned to her friend. "Did you ever have a man lick you that way?"

Tanisha's cheeks darkened. "Not with shots. But I did have a guy pour chocolate syrup on me once and lick it up."

"How was it?"

She grinned. "Sticky, but fun. We used half a can of the stuff before the evening was done." She laughed. "I had to throw the sheets out, though, they were such a mess." She glanced over to where the man was finishing up the last of the shot, to the applause of onlookers. "Liquor might not stain as bad."

"Hmm. I never thought I'd say this, but I sort of envy her."

"What? You want that bodybuilder licking shots off you?"

She laughed. "No. But look at her. The woman screams sex. No man ever tells her she looks too young or innocent to know what she really wants. I mean, I'd never have the nerve to have a guy do body shots on me in front of a bar full of people, but I can see how much of a turn on it might be."

"I get what you mean. Like one of those fantasies we have but would never do. Like getting it on with two guys at once."

"I bet she's done two guys at once."

"I bet she's done a guy and a girl at the same time. Maybe even two girls." Tanisha's eyes met hers. "You ever think about that? I mean, I'm not propositioning you or anything, I just want to know."

Erica shook her head. "No. Doesn't do anything with me. I'm pretty traditional in my fantasies." All she wanted was one guy. The man she was sure could satisfy all her desires. If only she could make him see that she could satisfy his.

10

"GOOD NEWS, you two." Carl strode into the broadcast booth in the middle of Erica's third week on the job. "According to the latest Arbitron ratings, the Hawk and Honey Show is second place in the four to 8:00 p.m. time slot in the Denver market. Up two places from last month."

"Guess our listeners prefer you to me on my own," Adam said to her. "Can't say I blame them."

"They prefer us together. Obviously we have smart listeners."

"Does this mean we get a raise?" Adam asked.

Carl narrowed his eyes. "It means you won't be looking for other work for a while at least." He slapped a stack of papers down on the console between them. "I have a new on-location gig for you two. Next Friday you'll be broadcasting from Outback Charlie's Bar and Grill, over on Kipling."

"Outback Charlie's?" Erica picked up a flyer featuring a cartoon parrot holding a mug of beer. "Never heard of it."

"It's a new place. The owner figured a promo with KROK was a natural. We're going to have you two set up there during happy hour, along with Ronnie."

"Ronnie?" Erica traded skeptical looks with Adam. "You're going to have a live alligator on location? Isn't that dangerous?"

"The bar owner's installing a sand pit and pool just for him. And there won't be any problems. Ronnie's a sweetheart." He turned to Adam. "In fact, we could have you get in the pit with Ronnie, show everybody he's harmless."

Erica bit her lip to keep from laughing at the horrified expression on Adam's face. "Absolutely not. No alligator wrestling."

"Not wrestling. Just tussle a little. Any injuries would be covered by workers' comp."

"No."

Carl shrugged. "It was just an idea." He consulted the papers again. "It'll be a beach theme, so we're talking swimsuits, sandals, sunglasses. Think party music. We'll have some contests. I'm thinking we can do rock trivia, so be coming up with some good questions, Adam."

"I can do that."

"Erica, I want you to come up with some games and activities to keep people entertained. Think beach party."

"So, like, a limbo contest or dance contest?"

"That's it." He gathered up the papers again. "One more thing. Bonnie's going to be on location with you. She'll do her regular weather and traffic updates, mingle with the crowds, stuff like that."

"Are you sure that's a good idea?" Adam said.

Carl gave him a sharp look. "Outback Charlie wants it. He's paying for it, so he gets her. That won't be a problem, will it?"

"Of course not." Adam's jaw tightened.

Carl nodded. "Good job, both of you. Keep it up. Next month I want to see number one in the drive-time slot."

"Sure thing," Adam said to Carl's retreating back. He turned to Erica. "A beach party. I can't wait."

"It'll be fun." She nudged his shoulder. "You remember how to loosen up and have fun, don't you?"

"Let's just say my idea of fun and Carl's aren't necessarily the same. For instance, mine doesn't include alligator wrestling. Or Bonnie."

"She'll be okay. She should be in a good mood, getting her share of the spotlight."

"You don't know her as well as I do. Bonnie wants all the spotlight to herself."

"And she'll have it. When she shows up in a bikini, nobody in that bar—at least none of the men—will be paying attention to you and me. We'll be able to do our show in peace."

His gaze flickered over her. "Don't sell yourself short. You'll be getting your share of attention, too, I don't doubt."

"From you?" She studied him through lowered lashes.

The lines on either side of his mouth deepened. "Right." Though his tone was less than enthusiastic, she didn't miss the way his eyes darkened, as if he was imagining her in a skimpy bathing suit.

"It'll be just like old times," she said. "You and me on location for a promo. Only instead of lingerie, I'll be wearing a swimsuit."

"But instead of a bed we'll have Bombshell Bonnie

and an alligator in a sandpit." He shook his head. "Somehow it won't be the same."

She lowered her voice. "I have a brand-new bed at my place, remember?"

His expression grew serious, and he held her gaze so long she felt a flush rise to her cheeks. "You never give up, do you?" he said.

She shook her head. "Not when I know you still want me the way I want you."

"How do you know that? I haven't said anything."

She put her hand on his chest, her fingertips brushing the triangle of hair showing at the open collar of his shirt. "You don't have to. It's in your eyes every time you look at me."

He turned his head away. "You're imagining things."

"Oh, I imagine lots of things." She dropped her voice to a whisper and leaned close, her lips almost brushing his ear. "I imagine you making love to me. Do you remember what it was like there, in the dark at the Furniture Gallery? How close we were? How it felt when you were in me?"

With a strangled noise, he turned away, and stormed out of the control booth, slamming the door behind him. She stared after him, hope fluttering in her chest. Adam might try to deny his feelings for her, but they were there. If she could only break past his fear of making a mistake.

AS PREDICTED, Bonnie showed up at Outback Charlie's wearing a gold lamé string bikini and gold high heels. A short, ruddy man with thinning brown hair, Charlie Mattingly, or Outback Charlie, rushed to greet her.

"Miss Remington, it's such a delight having you here with us," he said, taking her hand.

"I wouldn't have missed it." Bonnie looked around at the large wooden deck decorated with fake palm trees, neon flamingos and colorful beach umbrellas. "Cool place you have here."

"Could we get a picture together?" Charlie gestured toward one of the waiters, who held a digital camera.

"Sure." She posed with her arm around Outback Charlie, chest thrust forward. Then she obliged half a dozen other men with their own cheesecake photos.

"Hello, Bonnie," Adam said as he passed the photo session on his way to the stage set up at one end of the deck area, next to Ronnie's sandpit. The alligator hadn't moved since he'd been dropped off an hour ago. If Adam hadn't known better, he'd have sworn the animal was fake, another prop adding to the outback theme.

Bonnie lowered her sunglasses and surveyed his board shorts and blue and white Hawaiian shirt. "Didn't you get the memo. We're supposed to be in Australia, not Hawaii."

"Even Australians wear Hawaiian shirts."

Erica passed them. Today, she wore her hair in dozens of tiny braids. "Hi, Adam. Hello, Bonnie. What a great setup, huh?"

Sure. Great setup. For the next four hours I get to work between a woman with a hair trigger who hates my guts, and a woman I want more than I've wanted almost anything, except this job.

Bonnie lowered her sunglasses again. "Nice suit. Very…girlish."

Erica glanced down at the bright red one-piece with

deep cut-outs on each side. As far as Adam was concerned, that peekaboo suit was way more sexy than Bonnie's let-it-all-hang-out look. He was thankful for his own shades, so she couldn't see how he was staring at her. "Thanks, I like it." She flashed them both a smile and made her way past them to the stage. Adam followed her with his eyes, mesmerized by the way the red spandex clung to her perfect ass.

"Still mooning over Little Miss Muffet?" Bonnie nudged her sunglasses back into place.

He snapped his head toward her. "Leave her alone, Bonnie. I don't want to referee any cat fights."

She laughed. "What? You think we'd be fighting over *you?*" She swiveled away and spotted a quartet of workmen in the doorway. "Come on in, y'all." She beckoned them. "Say hello to Bombshell Bonnie."

He shook his head and joined Erica on stage. "What did I tell you?" Erica said. She nodded toward Bonnie and her adoring fans. "With Bonnie here, dressed like that, no one will even notice us."

"Not every man falls for fake boobs and teeny bikinis." He checked the setup for the speakers. "Some guys prefer a woman who leaves a little to their imagination."

"That's a sweet thing to say."

He glanced over his shoulder at her. "It's the truth."

"Thanks." She patted his shoulder. "You're good for my ego."

She picked up a box of T-shirts they used for giveaways and stepped off the stage. "I'll see if Bonnie wants to hand out some of these."

"Maybe you can talk her into wearing one."

She laughed. "Not a chance. She's enjoying show-ing off too much."

She left with the T-shirts and he returned to check-ing the speakers. One of the waiters, dressed in a blue Outback Charlie's polo shirt and black pants, ap-proached. "The boss wants to know if you need any-thing to eat or drink. On the house."

He looked up into a familiar face. He checked the name tag pinned to the polo. "Ray? Ray Kingston?"

"Hawk? Man, it *is* you." Ray crushed Adam's hand in his and shook it. "How you been?"

"I've been good? How are you?"

Ray shrugged and looked around the fake-Australian set. "Okay. I just started this job. Hope it works out."

Adam searched his face. How long had it been? Two years? Maybe closer to three. Ray was clean-shaven, a little more filled out than he remembered. "How long have you been in Denver?" he asked.

"Couple of months. I got a sister out here, talked me into coming out." He shrugged. "Thought it might be good to make a fresh start, you know? Took me a while to get a job, though. You know how it is."

"Yeah. I know." Adam hesitated, then asked. "You staying clean?"

Ray shoved his hands in his pockets, then took them out. "Yeah. I get tempted but my sister swore she'd turn me in herself if I got messed up." He glanced to-ward the door to the kitchen. "So, do you want anything to eat or drink? Don't want to give the new boss an ex-cuse to fire me the first day, you know?"

"Sure. I understand. Bring me a glass of iced tea when you get a chance."

"Coming right up."

Adam watched Ray go, and couldn't keep from smiling. It was good to see Ray doing so well. It reminded Adam again how lucky he was to be doing something he loved for a living, when he'd come so close to screwing it up.

His smile faded when, halfway across the room, Ray collided with Bonnie. "Watch where you're going!" she snapped.

Ray goggled at her and stammered an apology.

"What are you looking at?" she said. "Go on, get out of here."

Muttering about clumsy oafs, she joined Adam on the stage.

"If you're going to dress like that, you ought to get used to people staring," he said.

She fluffed her hair and adjusted the bikini top. "I don't see you staring."

He shook his head. "I've seen everything you have to offer and it doesn't do anything for me anymore."

He knew the minute the words were out that they were the wrong thing to say. Bonnie's eyes flashed with anger and he silently cursed his big mouth. "You just don't know how to handle a real woman," she said. "You'd rather have a girl, like—what did you call her?—effervescent Erica. Or do you prefer 'Honey'?"

He ground his teeth together, refusing to rise to her bait. "Are you ready to do the weather and traffic update at 4:10?"

She straightened her shoulders. "I'm always ready. I'm a professional."

Professional what? came to mind, but he didn't say it.

Ray returned with a glass of iced tea, steering clear of Bonnie, who was on the phone with the traffic helicopter.

Erica returned to the stage. "Are we ready to start?"

At 4:00 p.m. sharp they went live. "Good afternoon, everyone. We're coming to you live all afternoon from Outback Charlie's Bar and Grill at Kipling and Hampden. We've got two-for-one margaritas, great appetizers and dinner specials from Outback Charlie's fabulous grill, and we'll have plenty of music and cool prizes coming your way all afternoon. With me are the lovely Erica and Bombshell Bonnie with weather and traffic."

"Do you know how many men out there are jealous of you right now?" Erica asked. "Spending the afternoon with two hot women?"

"Get real," Bonnie said. "He could never handle both of us. After all, he couldn't handle me."

"I'll admit, I was no match for you, Bonnie. It takes a special man to put up with you."

She gave him a look that made clear she'd like nothing better than to take a sharp knife to certain sensitive body parts. He took an involuntary step back and killed her mic, just in case.

"We're all in awe of you, Bonnie." Erica rushed to defuse the moment. "What's the traffic like out there this afternoon?"

Adam gave her a grateful look and promised himself he'd avoid riling Bonnie any further.

When Bonnie finished her traffic and weather report, he addressed the crowd that had gathered. "Who wants to win some prizes?" he asked.

The two dozen or so people present cheered and whistled, egged on by Bonnie and Erica.

"All right. We're going to play a little rock 'n' roll trivia then. First right answer gets the new Ben Harper CD." He consulted the list of rock trivia questions he'd put together the night before. "What was Pat Benatar's job before she made it big?"

Erica took the remote mic into the audience. She approached a buff young construction worker who'd raised his hand. "Hey, handsome," she said, eliciting an immediate blush from the guy. "Do you know the answer?"

"Uh, is it…?"

She looked to Adam, who shook his head. "Sorry. Anybody else?"

After three tries, during which Adam played music, and the bathing-suit-clad Erica left three men tongue-tied, a man wearing an Avalanche shirt and jeans gave the correct answer of waitress and won the CD.

"All right, everybody!" Erica hopped back on stage and clapped her hands. "Time for our limbo contest. Line up for a chance to see how low you can go!" While Adam played "Don't worry 'bout a thing," she enlisted two audience members to hold a bamboo pole while she demonstrated the proper limbo technique. Back bent, hair almost touching the floor, she shimmied backward under the suspended pole while onlookers whooped and hollered. "If she had any boobs, she wouldn't be able to get down so low," Bonnie groused.

And if you had real boobs, you probably could, too. But again he resisted the temptation and kept his mouth shut.

After more music and giveaways, Bonnie instigated a hula contest. Remembering her earlier comment about his shirt, he silently wondered what was so Australian about the hula. In any case, she had an appreciative audience as she wiggled and swayed on the stage, and Outback Charlie himself came up to applaud her performance.

Music, weather, traffic, news. Before he knew it, they were halfway through the show. Ray approached him and Erica, order pad in hand. "Great show, guys. You ready for some dinner?"

"Sounds good. Ray, this is my co-host, Erica Gibson. This is an old friend of mine, Ray Kingston."

Erica offered her hand. "Nice to meet you, Ray."

"Same here." He gestured to the order pad. "So what can I get you? The burgers are good. So's the fish tacos."

"I'll try a burger," she said.

"Same here."

Ray noted their orders, then looked around. "What about the other lady?"

"Bonnie?" Adam looked around and spotted her at a table of businessmen. She was leaning over, signing autographs. The men weren't exactly drooling, but they were close. "She's over there at that table. Go ask her what she wants." At Ray's hesitant look he added, "Go on. She won't bite."

"Are you sure?" Erica asked when Ray had left.

"Not really." He picked up a list of e-mail addresses they'd collected from the audience and pretended to flip through it, trying not to notice how close she was standing, or how good she smelled, or how great her legs looked in her high-cut swimsuit. But he could feel her eyes on him.

"I like that shirt," she said. "Is that from your surfer days?"

Did she mean to remind him of the confidences they'd shared at the Furniture Gallery? "Nah, I bought this a couple of days ago for this gig. Thought I'd better look the part. Not that anyone is looking at me."

"No, they're all staring at Bonnie."

"Not all of them. I've caught a few eyes following you."

"What about you? Have you been looking at me?"

His eyes met hers. A mistake. Her gaze was steady, searching, asking more than her words implied. He cleared his throat. "Yes. I always look at you."

She licked her lips, sending heat slashing straight to his groin. "What do you think the chances would be of getting Carl to change his no-dating rule?"

"After what happened with Bonnie?" He shook his head. "Not a chance."

"It's not fair. We're adults. We ought to be able to do what we like after hours."

"It's what that can lead to on the air he's worried about."

"I'm not like Bonnie."

"Thank God."

At that moment, he was distracted by the bombshell herself. She'd retreated to an alcove, away from her fans, but her words carried to the stage. "You idiot. What do you mean interrupting me when I'm working? You've already annoyed me once today. Do it again and I'll see that you're fired."

Ray cowered before her, his order pad clutched to his chest. He stammered an apology, but Bonnie didn't hear.

Adam hurried to intervene. If Bonnie screwed things up for Ray, so help him he'd let her have it. She'd wish she'd never heard of the Hawk by the time he was through telling her exactly what he thought of her. "He was just trying to take our dinner orders." He took her arm and steered her away from the waiter.

"He interrupted me while I was talking to my fans," she said.

"An honest mistake. Now what do you want to eat?"

"A shrimp cocktail. And make sure the shrimp are fresh."

Adam nodded to Ray, who scribbled on his order pad, then hurried toward the kitchen. Bonnie glared after him. Great. He'd found the perfect hell, caught between a woman who hated his guts and another he wanted to love, but didn't dare.

ERICA SAW ADAM and Bonnie glaring at each other up on stage and felt the tension across the room. What was it with those two? Yes, Bonnie could be hard to deal with, but Adam needed to learn to handle her with kid gloves. Erica hurried forward to defuse the situation. "Bonnie, you were great during the hula contest," she said, inserting herself between her two co-workers. "Where did you learn to dance like that?"

Bonnie pulled her gaze away from Adam and smoothed her hair. "I never had a lesson. It's just knowing how to move your body."

"Maybe you could show me a few things sometime."

Bonnie looked her up and down. There was something predatory in the look that made Erica's skin crawl, but she kept a smile on her face. "Maybe I could."

She started to turn away, but Erica followed. "I've been wondering something," she said.

"What's that?"

"How did you get involved in radio? I mean, with your looks and…and your personality, you'd seem a natural for television."

The effect of the question was astonishing, Bonnie's expression softened and her smile seemed genuine. "You think so? I actually started out in television. A little station in Texas. I hosted a kiddie show." She giggled. "Can you believe it? But what I really wanted was to break into local news. I'd have been a perfect weather girl, don't you think?"

"You would." Erica could just see Bonnie, pointing out storm systems on a weather map while posturing for the camera.

"I was waiting for my chance when this guy I was dating offered me a place on his radio show. And I guess I put the TV stuff on hold for a while." She looked around the crowded restaurant. "This is kind of fun, though, don't you think? I like live appearances a lot better than being stuck in a studio, behind a mic."

"You're a natural."

"We're going to take a short break here, but enjoy the music and we'll be back shortly with more of the Hawk and Honey show with Bombshell Bonnie, live from Outback Charlie's Bar and Grill. Meanwhile, try one of Outback Charlie's dynamite Down Under specials like Shrimp Bloody Bay or Barrier Reef Fish Tacos."

"Let's go get some food," Erica said as Ray headed toward them carrying a loaded tray. "I'm starved."

Adam pulled a table close to the stage and helped Ray unload his tray. With shaking hands, the waiter placed the shrimp cocktail in front of Bonnie. "Is the shrimp fresh?" she asked, eyeing the dish suspiciously.

"I—I believe the shrimp were frozen. But I saw the cook boil them just for you."

"Frozen shrimp aren't fresh." She shoved the cocktail away. "Bring me some fresh ones."

Ray glanced at Adam and Erica, then looked back at Bonnie. "I don't think we have any fresh shrimp. Everything is frozen."

"Did I ask you to argue with me? Go get my order."

"Bonnie, stop it." Adam's voice cut through the tension. "The man can't serve you something that isn't on the menu."

"Is there a problem here?" Outback Charlie hurried to their table. "Is there something I can get you, Bonnie?"

"This waiter screwed up my order."

"He did not." Adam turned to Charlie. "Bonnie didn't know the shrimp were previously frozen."

"I asked for fresh. He told me it was fresh. He lied."

Ray opened his mouth to defend himself, but Charlie cut him off. "I warned you. One screwup and you were out the door. Now, go."

Adam stood abruptly. "He didn't do anything wrong." He glared at Bonnie. "Bonnie enjoys causing trouble."

"If he upset the lady, that's enough reason for me to let him go."

"Don't." Adam softened his voice, though his knuckles whitened around the fork he still held. "Give the guy a break. I can vouch for him."

Charlie looked surprised. "You know him?"

Adam nodded. "We've known each other for a few years." He glanced at Ray, whose expression had changed to wariness. "He's a good guy. You won't regret keeping him on."

"I don't know about that." He frowned at Ray. "I wanted to help a guy out, you know. But you worry with a guy like that. What if he starts stealing or something."

"I don't steal," Ray said. "I never stole."

Erica looked from one man to another. Something else was going on here, something more than Adam defending a waiter from Bonnie's wrath. What did Charlie mean *a guy like that?* Ray looked ordinary enough to her.

"Just because somebody has a record doesn't mean they'll steal or do anything else to jeopardize their job." The lines around Adam's mouth tightened. "Believe me, most people don't want to go back to jail."

"How do you know?" Charlie countered. "How many ex-cons who went straight do you know?"

"A few." He glanced at Ray again. The waiter was staring at him, eyes dark with hurt and anger. Adam looked at Charlie again. "Me, for instance. I was in prison with Ray, and I don't ever intend to go back. He doesn't, either, that's how I know you can trust him."

Erica stared at him, until the edges of her vision went gray. As if from a very long way away, she heard Bonnie gasp. "You're a con, too?" Charlie asked.

"An ex-con. I did my time and I've gone straight. Like Ray here."

Charlie shook his head. "Who'd've thought?" He gave Adam a hard look. "I never heard you say anything about that on the radio."

"It's not the kind of thing that comes up much in casual conversation."

Charlie looked at Ray again. "Okay. One more chance. Don't blow it."

"Thanks." He spoke through clenched teeth. Erica wondered how much pride he swallowed to say it. With a stiff nod, he left their table.

Adam sat back down and picked up his burger. No one else moved.

He put the burger back down. "What?"

"You were in prison?" Bonnie was clearly horrified. "You never told me."

"It was none of your business." He glanced at Erica, then back at Bonnie. "It was in California, before I came here. It's over."

"Oh God." She sprang from the table and fled.

Charlie stood. "I'll go see if she's all right."

When the two of them were alone, Erica tried to eat, but she couldn't get the haunted look in Ray's eyes out of her head. Had Adam ever looked like that? She pushed her plate aside. "That was really something," she said. "You sticking up for Ray that way."

He popped a French fry into his mouth and chewed, a closed expression on his face. "Go ahead and ask."

"Ask what?" She flushed.

"The six million dollar question. What was I in for?"

"Okay. What were you in for?"

"Drugs. Coke. Blow. I had a big habit back then. Dealt some on the side. It was a big mistake."

"That was what you were talking about, when you said you got in big trouble at your last job?"

He nodded. "Nobody wanted me to work for them when I got out. Carl gave me a chance." His eyes met hers. "So you see why I can't mess it up."

"I see." She looked at her lap. She loved Adam partly because he was hardworking and a straight-arrow and... and decent. But those same qualities were also the ones keeping them apart.

Adam didn't want to screw up. Which left her... screwed.

11

SILENCE STRETCHED between Erica and Adam like a high tension wire about to snap. He struggled to come up with something to say to get them back to the easy friendship they'd known. This was why he hadn't told her this part of his past before. She'd never look at him the same way again. He understood, but that didn't make it any easier to take.

She pushed her chair back and stood, not looking at him. "I think I'll go freshen up before we go back on air."

He watched her leave, a sick feeling in his stomach. He'd wanted to put some distance between them, and revealing his past had done the trick. But he hadn't imagined how much her rejection would hurt. He'd wanted to think she was different, that what he did or what he'd been didn't matter as much as who he was inside.

No such luck.

He wrapped up the uneaten quarter of his burger and took it to the trash. He wouldn't be surprised if Charlie didn't try to call off the rest of the gig. Carl would go ballistic. Adam would be lucky to keep his job.

His lips formed a tight smile. Wouldn't that be ironic? If Carl let him go, he'd be free to date Erica. Except that after today, she probably wouldn't want anything to do with him.

Mason sent a note that it was time for them to go back on the air. Adam put on his headset and prepared to wow the audience with classic Hawk persona—the trivia God, the thinker, the man for whom music was his life.

"Welcome back to this special edition of the Hawk and Honey show on KROK. We're broadcasting live from Outback Charlie's Bar and Grill. Bombshell Bonnie is here with me and Erica, so stop by and say hello. Enjoy the great food and drinks from Outback Charlie's and participate to win some prizes."

A rowdy group of five men entered and took a table near the stage. They waved and called to Bonnie, who made her way to their table. "Hello, boys," she drawled in her best Mae West imitation. "Did y'all come out to see me?"

"We sure did, gorgeous." One of the men stood and began dancing to the music. "Let's dance."

Bonnie obliged, doing an exaggerated bump and grind that had all the tables around her cheering. Erica joined Adam on stage. "How long before she does a table dance?" she asked.

He shook his head. "I never put anything past Bonnie."

She leaned closer, her voice low. "Hey, you okay?"

Why was she asking? Did he not look okay? "What do you mean?"

"You seem kind of distracted."

Who wouldn't be? But maybe she thought he was supposed to be Mr. Cool all the time. A hard case. Nothing ever affected him. "I'm fine."

"I thought maybe what happened at dinner upset you."

"Why would it upset me?" *I only spilled my guts, shocked my so-called friends into silence and jeopardized my job.*

She shrugged. "You know, brought back bad memories or something."

She didn't know the half of it. But it wasn't memories that dogged him. It was frustration about the future. Was his past always going to affect the rest of his life? Without a record hanging over his head, would he have risked an affair with Erica? He might have. Maybe he'd have faced down Carl and told him his no-dating rule was stupid and unfair. Or maybe he'd have had the confidence to get a job at another station if Carl fired him.

Now that she knew Adam was an ex-con, was Erica even still interested in him? Her sudden coolness at the dinner table after his revelation told him she probably wasn't. "I'm fine," he said again.

She gave him a puzzled look and turned away. "That was Jack Johnson," she announced. "Happy hour's in full swing here at Outback Charlie's, so come on down and join us. We've got two-for-one margaritas, Foster's beer and appetizers. And the KROK crew will be here until seven o'clock giving away prizes and playing music."

"I'm going to take a break," he told her, and headed off the stage. Ray stopped him outside the men's room. He'd changed out of his Outback Charlie's polo into a black button-down shirt. "Are you leaving?" Adam asked. Had his big confession been a complete waste? Had Charlie fired Ray after all?

"My shift's over. Thanks for taking up for me this afternoon. If it weren't for you, I'd be out of a job."

"You didn't do anything wrong. I couldn't let that slide."

"Sure you could have. Big radio personality. You didn't have to tell everyone you'd done time."

Adam rubbed the back of his neck, where a headache was building. "Yeah, well, it's part of my life. You don't ever really leave it behind."

"Tell me about it. So, everything cool? I mean, with your job and everything?"

"It's all right." He clapped Ray on the shoulder. "Hang in there."

"I will. You, too."

They said goodbye and he stood in the hallway outside the rest-rooms and looked toward the stage. Erica was leading the audience in a singalong to "Margaritaville." She looked fantastic, dancing around the stage, her face lit by a smile. Watching her, he felt a hollowness in his gut.

Like the ache he had sometimes when he was doing drugs—a wanting so strong he couldn't fight it. Back then it meant he'd go out and score another hit. But he couldn't do that with Erica. He had Carl to think about, and the repercussions of the revelation he'd made at dinner.

Worse, a bad feeling dogged him, one he couldn't push away. What if she didn't want him anymore?

BY THE TIME they finished at Outback Charlie's and headed back to the station, Erica had moved from shocked to sad to outright annoyed. Ever since his big revelation about his past, Adam had said hardly two words to her. As if, now that she knew this about him, he was determined to shut her out even further.

Maybe Tanisha was right. Maybe Adam had problems Erica couldn't solve. Maybe he wasn't worth wasting so much emotional energy on.

But what about those magic moments in the dark at the Furniture Gallery? She'd seen another side to the aloof intellectual then. She'd discovered a man of great tenderness and passion. A man she wasn't ready to let go.

She pulled into the parking lot of KROK and sat staring at the building. Adam had gone straight home. Bonnie was probably still flirting with Outback Charlie. That left Erica to drop off the list of e-mail addresses and other paperwork from the gig. Not that she minded. The last thing she wanted right now was to go home to her empty apartment, where she'd do nothing but worry about Adam.

Would he be at home worrying about her? Or was he truly that rare person who preferred to be alone? He had cultivated that image, but, having glimpsed another side of him at the Furniture Gallery, she wasn't so sure.

There had to be some way to get through to him. Damn Carl's stupid rule. What job was worth being miserable during your time off? She got out of the car and headed toward the building, an idea growing in her mind. If she wasn't having any luck pursuing Adam at work, maybe it was time to move to less neutral territory. Away from work, he wouldn't be able to hide behind the microphone, or use their unseen listeners as an excuse for not admitting his true feelings.

With this in mind, she headed down the stairs, where she found Tanisha packing up to head home. "I hope you haven't shut down your computer yet," Erica said.

Tanisha looked up from stuffing papers into an overflowing tote bag. "I have. Why?"

"I need you to find Adam's home address for me."

"I'm not supposed to give out employees' personal information," she said, even as she hit the button to reboot her computer.

"I won't tell a soul." She dragged a chair over beside Tanisha's and studied the monitor.

"So what's up with you two?" Tanisha said. "On air, everything sounds copasetic."

Erica shook her head. "On the air, we get along great. But he refuses to have anything to do with me outside of the show."

"Wait a minute. I thought you two really hit it off." The desktop screen came up and she selected the database program.

"We did. Even he admits that. But there's Carl's stupid rule about on-air personalities not dating."

Tanisha nodded. "He doesn't want to risk his job. Something maybe you should think about."

"I've thought about it, and I still don't see why I can't have the job I want *and* the man I want."

"So this is really all about you." Tanisha looked amused.

Erica squirmed in her chair. "So I'm selfish. What's so bad about that?" She'd been called worse in her life. And it could be said her impulsiveness stemmed from a desire for immediate gratification. "But it's about Adam, too. He's not happy." Watching him go through the motions of doing the show after his big confession at dinner, she'd wanted more than anything to throw her arms around him and tell him everything was all right. She could see him putting up walls, determined to be so damned *strong*. It hurt to think he didn't feel he could be himself, even around her.

"And you think you could make him happy?" Tanisha asked.

Erica nodded. "We could make each other happy."

Tanisha scrolled through a list of records, and clicked on Adam's name. "So what are you going to do—go out to his house and demand he sleep with you?"

"I'm going to demand he talk to me. Really talk." Of course, the only time Adam let down his guard was in bed. "If that leads to other things…that would be fine with me."

"Okay, here's the addy. Twenty-one forty-three Clarkson. That's in Morrison."

Erica snatched a sheet of paper from the printer and scribbled the address. "Thanks."

"Sure. Buy me a drink later."

"We could get together tomorrow night."

"Uh-uh. I've got plans." A knowing smile tugged at her lips.

"What kind of plans?"

"I'm going to take your advice, and try that little harem girl outfit out on my new guy."

Erica laughed. "Then you will be busy. Have fun."

"You, too."

Erica debated going home to change clothes, but decided to head straight to Adam's, before she lost her nerve. After consulting a map and making a couple of wrong turns, she found his home on a quiet street tucked beneath a red rock cliff. She pulled into the driveway behind his Jeep and cut the engine.

She hoped she was doing the right thing. After to-night, Adam would either accept the fact that there was a connection between them worth exploring, or he would shut her out of his life altogether.

She checked her hair in the rearview mirror, then got out of the car and made her way up the front walk. She rang the bell and waited. And waited. Frowning, she rang again, and tried to peer in the window beside the door. His Jeep was in the driveway, so he had to be home, right? Unless he'd gone out with a friend. A date, even...

The thought made her feel queasy. Maybe she *was* making a mistake coming here. What if she'd misread him? What if their so-called "connection" was entirely one-sided? What if this *was* all about her and there was no *them?*

She almost fell as the door was jerked open and Adam stood there, dripping wet, clad only in a towel around his waist. "Erica? What are you doing here?"

She tried to ignore the way water droplets sparkled in his chest hair, or the wet sheen of his muscular shoulders. Her gaze involuntarily dropped to the towel. A rather small towel. Not really large enough to cover much...

"Erica? Is something wrong?"

Only lust jamming all my brain cells. She managed a weak smile. "You and I need to talk."

His mouth tightened, but after a moment's hesitation, he nodded. "You'd better come in."

She followed him into a dimly lit living room. A pair of black leather sofas faced each other across an oriental rug. An entertainment center, complete with a big-screen TV, filled one wall, while a rock fireplace sat between floor to ceiling windows on the opposite wall. "Nice place," she said.

"Make yourself at home. I'll go get dressed." He headed toward a doorway leading to the rest of the house, his bare feet slapping against the hardwood floor.

"Don't go to any trouble on my account," she called after him. "What you have on looks fine to me."

While he was gone, she looked around the room. It was comfortable, classy even. She trailed her finger through the dust on the mantel. Definitely a bachelor pad. A bookcase in one corner held a collection of popular novels, rock history books and a few outdoor guides. The magazines on the coffee table ranged from *Rolling Stone* to *Backpacker*. But there were no photographs anywhere. In fact, the walls were mostly bare, except for a single watercolor over one sofa, the kind of thing you might buy at any furniture store, a last-minute accessory purchased without much thought.

She was seated on one of the sofas, flipping through an old issue of *Guitar* magazine when he returned. He'd changed into jeans and a cotton shirt that he left untucked. He was still barefoot. His hair was damp, curling up at the neckline of his shirt. He reminded her of the way he'd been at the Furniture Gallery. Casual. Relaxed.

He sat on the sofa opposite her. "What do you think we need to talk about that we haven't already said?"

"You've done a lot of talking, but I don't feel like you've really listened to me." She got up and crossed over to sit beside him. "And I have some questions for you."

He crossed his arms over his chest and frowned at her. "I'm not promising I'll answer."

"Those nights we spent together at the furniture gallery, after everyone else was gone, I felt so close to you. Even when we were only talking, I saw a side of you you'd never revealed at work." She looked around the room, at the comfortable furniture but lack of real personal details. "You seemed to really relax with me, more than you do at the station, where you've always kept to yourself. Why is that, do you think?"

"You're an easy person to be with." He uncrossed his arms and rested his hands on his thighs. "And I'm probably not as uptight when I'm turned on."

"So you admit I turn you on." She leaned toward him, her tone teasing.

The heat that flared in his eyes was unmistakable. "I don't think there's ever been any doubt of that."

She put her hand on his thigh and began moving slowly up and down. She felt him tense, but he didn't try to move away. "So which is the real Adam Hawkins? Is he the intellectual loner I first met at the station? Is he 'the Hawk,' the rock history expert and glib radio personality people hear on the air?" She turned and looked into his eyes, pinning him with her gaze. "Or is he the sexy, passionate guy I met under the covers at the Furniture Gallery?" She stopped her hand at the top of his thigh, the tips of her fingers almost, but not quite brushing against the fly of his jeans.

He put his hand on her shoulder. "Maybe I'm all those people."

"But am I the only one who sees all those sides of you? I think right now, at least, I am." She left her hand where it was, and brought the other up to rest on his chest. She could feel his heart beating, a steady pulsing against her palm.

"That doesn't change things. We still work together on the air. Trying to be a couple off the air is risky."

"I've never been one to be afraid of risk." She leaned toward him, until her breath brushed his neck. "I think it would be much worse to risk losing that passionate, *real* Adam Hawkins to the other images you project." She rested her lips against his throat and closed her eyes, waiting for his answer.

"You don't know what you're getting into, Erica. Seriously."

"Then tell me. That's why I'm here."

He closed his eyes. He wanted to say the hell with it all and pick her up and carry her into the bedroom. But caution built up over the years held him back.

"I don't expect you to say anything. I just want you to see where I'm coming from. While I was in prison, I enrolled in a rehab program. I kicked my habit. I thought I'd be able to go back to my old life. Only this time I wouldn't screw up like before."

"So you came to Denver to start over?"

"No, I came to Denver because KROK was the only place that would even give me an interview. Station managers took one look at my record—which I was required by law to tell them about—and said no way do we want to mess with this joker."

"That's horrible."

"All I needed was one chance, and Carl gave it to me." His eyes met hers. "I don't intend to waste it."

She rose and stood in front of him. "Did you think it would matter to me, that you'd been in prison?"

"I'd be surprised if it didn't."

"We all make mistakes. Some of them bigger than others." She put her arms around his neck and kissed him.

He'd told himself kicking a drug habit had equipped him to resist any temptation. But he hadn't bargained on the intoxicating pull of acceptance, or the power of longing to forget about everything in a willing woman's arms.

"We shouldn't do this," he said, even as he returned the kiss, letting the pressure of his lips against hers and the sweep of his tongue say all the things he didn't have words for.

When they broke apart, he fought to keep his breathing even, to control the emotion that threatened to overwhelm him. Her eyes met his, her expression tender. "If we don't do it, won't you regret it? Would you really rather be alone than be with me?"

He'd been alone too long. All his caution had brought him nothing but too much loneliness. "What about Carl?" he asked.

"I think we have a couple of choices there. We can try to keep our relationship a secret. No one at work needs to know about it. Or we can go to Carl, tell him…tell him we have feelings for each other, and that he needs to accept that."

"And if he doesn't accept it?"

She took a deep breath. "Then we find other jobs. We're the number two rated show in the afternoon drive slot in Denver, on our way to number one. That ought to be worth something."

He tightened his hands on her waist. "It's a big risk."

"A big risk is worth it for a big payoff."

He looked into her eyes. There was no accusation there, no suspicion. Only a wanting that reflected his own feelings. He didn't want to fight her anymore—to fight himself. Better to give in to his feelings and deal with the consequences than continue this painful struggle. "Let's go into the bedroom," he said.

She smiled up at him. "I thought you'd never ask."

12

ERICA FOLLOWED Adam into his bedroom. Like the rest of his house, this room was masculine and comfortable—dark wood furniture, a navy-blue comforter on the queen-size bed, a leather armchair piled with magazines and old clothes in one corner. He picked up a pair of jeans from the floor and flung them into the chair. "If I'd know you were coming, I'd have cleaned up."

"It's okay. I'd have been disappointed if it was neater than my own place."

He came up behind her and put his arms around her and began kissing her neck. She leaned against him and closed her eyes. If people could purr, she'd being doing so right now.

"Turn around and look at me." He turned her toward him.

She pressed her palm to his cheek. His skin was smooth, clean-shaven. When he closed his eyes his lashes tickled her fingertips. "This is different, isn't it?" she said. "With the lights on, being able to see each other."

"You don't know how much I've wanted to see you. All of you." His gaze swept over her. "Those times when I missed my cues when we were on air? It was usually because I was sitting there, imagining you naked."

The thought of him fantasizing about her made her stomach flutter. She stepped back and held out her arms, smiling. "Then be my guest."

He studied her a moment, as if deciding where to start first. She began to feel a little silly, standing there with her arms outstretched. Then he reached for the top button of her blouse. "I was debating how upset you'd be if I didn't waste time unbuttoning these, but just ripped the shirt off."

"Don't." She put her hand over his and looked into his eyes. "Let's take our time. Really get to know each other." More than anything, she wanted him to trust her, to realize he didn't have to hide anything from her.

He reached for the next button and undid it, then moved to the next.

"You're still going too fast," she said.

"I am?" He looked puzzled.

She smiled. "You want to take the time to really appreciate the moment. Like this." She carefully unfastened the top button of his shirt, then leaned forward and kissed the triangle of chest that had been revealed. She swirled her tongue over his skin and breathed in his clean scent. Then she moved on to the next button, pausing to kiss each newly exposed inch of bare skin, down his chest, to his stomach, moving slowly, exploring him thoroughly. She circled her tongue around his navel and he drew a sharp breath, and his hands tightened on her shoulders.

Encouraged, she moved lower, tracing her tongue along the line of fine hair leading to the waistband of his jeans. She followed with her fingers, stroking his abdomen, teasing along the top of his jeans. "I want to make sure every inch of you is aware of me," she said. "Wanting me."

"Uh-huh. You're doing a great job."

Just as every inch of her was attuned to him, aware of the rhythm of his breathing, and the way the fine hairs lay on the back of his hand, of the scar on his knuckle and the hint of a dimple on the right side of his mouth. She was coming to know him so well, and yet there was so much more she wanted to know.

"Let's get in bed," she said. She took his hand and tugged back the comforter with the other. Then she lay back against the pillows.

He stopped to strip off his jeans and the unbuttoned shirt, leaving him naked. "Not that I'm impatient, or anything," he said as he tossed the clothes aside. "I thought I'd get more comfortable."

He was very erect. Watching him move toward her she felt a renewed tension between her legs. An aching to have him in her. But not yet. There was more she wanted to know about him, and the intimacy of sex seemed to be the only time he let down his guard enough to say them. For instance, he hadn't wanted to talk about his time in prison. "Did you think about sex a lot when you were in prison?" she asked.

He knelt on the bed and frowned at her. "Why do you ask?"

"I want to know about you. What it was like for you." She smoothed her hand down his arm, the muscles hard beneath her palm.

He lay down and pulled her toward him, his head

resting alongside hers. She could no longer see his face, but she could feel the heat of his naked body, pressed against her. "Yeah, I thought about it," he said, his voice low in her ear. "I mean, there weren't any women around, and when you can't have something, you automatically think about it more." He kissed her again, his lips crushing hers, his tongue thrusting deep into her mouth, as if he wanted to devour her, or silence her questions.

She arched against him, reveling in the feel of him, but when his mouth moved to her neck, she drew back slightly, determined to continue the conversation. "Did you have a girlfriend when you went in?"

He shook his head. "No one in particular. No one waiting for me, if that's what you mean."

She trailed her hand along his hip, her touch light. Teasing. "So what did you think about doing?"

"What do you mean?"

She raised her head and looked into his eyes. "Tell me your fantasies. The things no one else knows."

He swallowed hard, was silent for a moment. "I can't think. All the blood's rushed south."

She squeezed his buttocks, and watched his cock jerk in response. "What did you do to relieve the tension. Did you masturbate?"

He choked back a laugh. "Yeah. Guys do that all the time anyway."

"So do women. At least some of them. I do." She looked up at him again. "Lately, I've been thinking about you when I do it."

His eyes darkened and his breathing grew uneven.

"That makes you hot, doesn't it?" She dropped her

hand to cover her crotch. "Thinking about me getting myself off?"

"Yeah, it does."

She wet her lips, and hesitated over the next question. But she wanted them to be honest with each other. For him to know there was nothing he couldn't tell her. "There are a lot of stories about prison life. About men, locked up all that time together, things they do…"

The muscles beneath her hand tensed into hard ridges. He took a deep breath and she felt him relax slightly. "If you're asking did I ever have sex with another man, no. Some guys did, but I didn't. And if you're worried about disease or anything, I'm clean."

"I wasn't worried. Just curious." She kissed his neck, resting her lips against the hollow at the base of his throat. "You can tell me anything and I promise I won't judge. I just want to know."

"Now it's my turn to ask you a question."

Her eyes widened. "Uh, sure. What is it?"

He fingered one thin blond braid. "What's with your hair? Every time I see you lately, you're wearing it a different way."

She shrugged. "I guess I get bored with it. I like to change it up. You don't like it?"

"I like it fine. I just wondered." He began undoing her shirt again. "I'm supposed to be undressing you, aren't I?" He followed her lead this time and lingered over the job. He pulled down the top of the swimsuit and trailed his tongue over the valley between her breasts and she closed her eyes against the sheer pleasure of the contact.

She opened her eyes again, determined not to get

carried away too soon. She laced her fingers through his hair, surprised at how soft it was when it looked so coarse. "Did you have to wear your hair cut short in prison?"

He sighed. Was he annoyed at her questions? Or resigned to answering them? "Not really. We had to wear these orange pajama pants and pullover tops. And rubber sandals." He pulled back and propped himself on one elbow, his gaze searching. "Why are you so interested? Is this some kind of a turn-on for you, knowing I was locked up?"

She smiled. "Think of it as a kind of foreplay." She sat up and squeezed his arm. "I want to know what it was like. I want you to know it's okay to talk about anything with me. To let out the feelings you've kept locked up inside."

He looked away. "Feelings are dangerous. Emotions take over, you stop thinking and do stupid stuff."

The anger in his voice startled her. When had he ever done anything stupid? "Like with Bonnie?"

"Not Bonnie." He looked at her again, his gaze probing, as if he wanted to make sure she understood what he was saying. "There wasn't any real feeling there. I think that's why I slept with her in the first place. She was safe. She didn't care enough about me to dig deep."

And I do. Did he understand how much she cared? "Then what are you talking about? When have you done something stupid because you let emotion take over?"

He sat up, and rested his elbows on his knees. He was naked and she was still half-dressed, their passion subdued in exchange for a different kind of intimacy.

"In California, I had a best friend. Another jock at the station where I worked. We were roommates for a while, we hung around together, even dated some of the same women. He…he was kind of like a brother to me."

She touched his arm, wanting to reassure him. "Was he into drugs, too?"

"Oh, yeah. He's the one who turned me on to them. Introduced me to his dealer. I thought it was because we were such good friends."

"What happened?"

"They picked him up for something, he had a kilo of coke with him. He'd been popped before, so he was looking at hard time. His lawyer cut a deal. If he'd reveal his sources, they'd go easy on him."

"So he turned in the dealer?"

He shook his head. "No. He knew if he did that, he'd end up dead. So he told them I was his source."

The hurt in his eyes as he remembered this betrayal pained her. "Did you ever get a chance to ask him why?"

"He said he was doing me a favor. He was teaching me a valuable lesson in life—trust no one."

"He was wrong." She knelt in front of him, her voice insistent. "You have to trust someone some time. Otherwise, you're always…alone."

"Yeah, well, it hasn't been that bad. Until you came along. You made me start thinking differently. That night in the Furniture Gallery. When we talked…" He shook his head. "I couldn't believe the stuff I said to you. Stupid stuff, like about my father…"

"It wasn't stupid. It was real. It made me feel…connected to you. You felt it, too, didn't you?"

"Yeah. Scared the shit out of me."

"Are you scared now?"

His eyes met hers, doubt in his expression. "Honest? I am…a little."

She nodded. "I am, too. I think that means these feelings are real. Don't run away from them."

He lay back, and pulled her down alongside him. "I'm not running anywhere. I'm staying right here with you."

Together, they got rid of her shirt, then her skirt and the swimsuit. He raised up on one elbow and looked at her, his hand tracing the curve of her hip. "You're beautiful."

It was something men said at a time such as this, but something a woman never got tired of hearing. "The way you look at me—you make me feel beautiful."

He scooted down and kissed her left breast, making circles with his tongue, drawing closer and closer to, but never touching, her erect nipple. She arched against him, craving his mouth on that sensitive peak. She felt him smile against her breast, then he scraped his teeth across her, making her gasp.

His tongue followed, soothing the ache, then his teeth made her more sensitive still. She moaned and clutched at his shoulders. "Do you want me to stop?" he asked, his lips still pressed against her.

"No. No, don't stop."

He moved to her other breast, alternately caressing and abrading until her vision fogged and she gasped for breath, certain a single touch to her clit would send her over the edge.

He rested his forehead between her breasts, his eyes

closed, mouth twisted in almost a grimace. "What's wrong?" she asked, alarmed.

He smiled. "Nothing. Just…catching my breath." He squeezed her thigh. "Don't want everything to be over before we've started."

It moved her that she wasn't the only one having trouble maintaining control. She nudged him onto his back, then sat up and straddled him. She could feel his erection, hot and hard between her thighs, nudging at her entrance. "So tell me what you want."

"You know what I want."

"Tell me." She squeezed her thighs together, encouraging him.

"I want my cock inside you." He raised up on his elbows. "I want to suck your nipples and squeeze your ass while you ride me until I come. And I want to make you come, hard. I want to hear you moan and cry my name and beg me not to stop."

She swallowed hard, shaken by the image his words painted. "I think we can manage that." She grabbed a condom from the nightstand and quickly sheathed him.

She was wet, her thighs trembling on the edge of control as she held herself over him, making herself wait, prolonging the moment. Then she guided him inside her, her muscles contracting around him. She pushed down, driving him deep, gasping at the sensation of him filling her.

He smoothed his hands over her buttocks, grasping and kneading. She tightened around him even more, the hard bud of her clit throbbing with every stroke of his cock.

She put her hands on either side of his head and

leaned forward. He raised his head from the pillow and took one nipple in his mouth, sucking hard, sending a renewed wave of wet heat to wrap around him as she rocked back and forth.

"Do you like that?" he asked, before transferring his mouth to her other nipple.

"Uh-huh." The sensation left her wordless, reduced to grunts and moans, all focus on his hands and mouth on her, and his hard cock inside her.

His mouth was busy adoring her breasts, while his hands caressed her bottom. She braced herself more firmly and brought her own hand to stroke her clit with her thumb, her fingers spread to brush against his erection with each stroke.

He took his mouth from her breast and watched. "It drives me crazy, watching you touch yourself that way."

"I like watching you watch me. That glazed look you get in your eyes, like any minute you'll lose control."

"That's the idea, isn't it? To make me lose control?"

"Yeah. And I'll be right there with you." She drove down harder, thrusting him deeper inside her, then withdrew almost all the way.

He grabbed her buttocks and pulled her toward him, arching to meet her, guiding her into a faster rhythm. She moved with him, no longer in control, every nerve focused on her approaching climax. She grit her teeth, reaching for it, white light exploding behind her tightly shut eyes as release came in rolling waves. She was dimly aware of him pulsing within her, his hands gripping her tightly as his groans filled her ears.

He wrapped his arms around her and hugged her tightly to his chest. They lay without speaking, their breath gradually growing more even, their hearts slowing to a steady beat. She thought he might have fallen asleep, when he spoke. "That was worth waiting for."

"Yeah." She eased away from him and over to his side, her arm across his chest, her head nestled in the hollow of his shoulder. "But I'm glad we decided not to wait any longer."

He caressed her shoulder. "What are we going to do about Carl?"

"We probably should talk to him, but…"

"But what?"

She raised her head to look at him. "But even if he doesn't fire us, he'll make a big fuss and everyone at the station will know. It would be nice if we could enjoy ourselves without all that hassle. At least for a while."

"Yeah. Let's just play it cool and see what happens."

"Maybe if we can prove that our having a relationship won't interfere with our jobs, he'd agree to relax the rule."

"And if he doesn't?"

She laid her head back on his shoulder. "Then we'll deal with it when the time comes. Together."

ADAM LAY AWAKE a long time after Erica's breathing had changed to the soft, even rhythm of sleep. If he closed his eyes and gave in to the lethargy that pulled at him, would he wake to find this whole evening had been a dream?

He couldn't remember feeling this close to anyone— ever. The idea was both thrilling and terrifying. She wanted so much from him—honesty and revelations about his past. Things he wasn't used to giving.

He'd spent so many years avoiding getting too close to anyone. Letting down his guard felt dangerous.

But having her here right now felt too good to give up. Answering her questions and seeing the acceptance in her eyes made him feel…clean. Renewed, somehow.

Is that why sex with her was different? More intense? More physical and more emotional, too?

Could that feeling possibly last? When Carl found out about them, as he would eventually—there were no real secrets in a workplace as small as a radio station—would he fire them? Would they become rivals for the limited number of radio spots available in a city the size of Denver?

She sighed softly and snuggled closer to him. He tightened his fingers around her shoulder, as if holding on to her would help him hold on to the faith she had in their future.

13

"YOU'RE LISTENING to the Hawk and Honey show on KROK, Denver's home for Today's Rock. That was U2 with 'All Because of You.'" Adam nodded to Erica, her signal to begin the next commercial.

"Summer is certainly in full swing here in Denver." Hot enough, in fact, that she'd taken to wearing her hair piled up on her head. "For all your refrigeration and air-conditioning needs, call on Front Range Refrigeration. They're an authorized Carrier dealer and can have you cooled off in no time." She made a show of fanning herself, and unbuttoned the top button of her shirt. Once she knew she had Adam's attention, she winked at him. "Maybe we should give them a call, Hawk. Does it feel warm in here to you?"

"I'm hot, all right, but I don't think it has anything to do with the weather." His voice was a sexy growl that melted her from the inside out.

"Then I'll just have to see what I can do about cooling you off," she purred, and hit the button to play the next song.

He ripped off his headset and rolled his chair closer to her. "I don't think a song is going to cool me off," he said softly.

"Mmm, maybe what you need is a tongue-lashing. I could get you nice and wet. Would that cool you off?" She looked toward the ceiling, miming innocence.

"You like to torture me that way, don't you?" He slipped his hand under her skirt, stroking the top of her thigh.

She caught her breath. "Careful," she warned, glancing toward the windows that looked out over the KROK offices.

"No one can see my hand. Only your face." He nudged one finger under the leg opening of her panties. "Just make sure they can't see by your face what I'm doing." He slid his finger lower, parting her folds.

"That's not fair," she whispered, gritting her teeth, to keep from moaning.

He grinned. "But you started it." He pulled his hand away and rolled his chair back, as far from her as the small booth allowed. His face was flushed and, in spite of his nonchalance, he was breathing hard.

"We must be crazy," she muttered. "I can hardly keep my hands off you."

"And I obviously can't keep my hands off you." He slid the finger that had been touching her into his mouth and drew it out slowly. She clenched her thighs together and swallowed hard, then realized it was time for the station identification. "You're listening to KROK, 97.8. The station that rocks Denver."

She smiled to herself as she made the announcement. Her and Adam's on-air routine of sexy banter and flirtation lent an extra edge to the workday. After four hours trading double entendres and teasing looks, they were both so hot there were days when they barely made it into the house before they started tearing off each other's clothes.

Listeners must have liked the extra spicy version of the Hawk and Honey show as well. In the past month, they'd captured the number one rating in the Denver market. All the more reason for Carl to repeal his stupid rule and let them date openly.

But neither of them was ready to test that theory yet. For now, it was more fun to keep their relationship secret, to play sexy games on air and spend erotic nights together.

She was getting a fast lesson in what those ratings meant. Almost overnight, it seemed she was a local celebrity. Not only was her voice on the air four hours every weekday, but also her picture was on billboards all over town, alongside Adam. People had begun to recognize her in the grocery store or restaurants. She'd even been asked for her autograph a few times, something that still amazed her.

Tanisha was the only one who knew about her relationship with Adam, and Erica trusted her not to blab. Tanisha was having her own hot and heavy romance with the man from her building, and the two friends often spent lunch hours comparing notes.

"So, is Adam a little more talkative now that you two are lovers?" Tanisha asked as they waited in line at a local deli one lunch hour.

"He's not the most emotional man I ever dated, but when we're alone, he doesn't mind telling me things. He even volunteers stuff sometimes." Just the other night, he'd told her about his days as "Airwave" Adam on his college radio station, and the outrageous stunts he and the other interns had pulled. He'd shown her a sharp sense of humor she'd only glimpsed before. "I think he's starting to trust me more. He's been burned in the past. So that's something." She picked up her tray and followed Tanisha toward a booth along the back wall of the restaurant. "What about you and Bryan? How's that going?"

"It's going great." A smile spread across Tanisha's face. "Last night he told me he loved me."

"Oh wow. That's so great." She reached across to squeeze Tanisha's hand. "I'm so happy for you."

"What about Adam? Has he used the L word yet?"

She shook her head and stabbed at her salad. "I haven't told him I love him, either. I don't want to scare him off." But every time they were together, her longing to hear that he loved her grew.

"Maybe he's waiting for you to say it first," Tanisha said.

"I've come close, but somehow, it never seems like the right time."

"Excuse me, but aren't you Erica Gibson, from the Hawk and Honey show?"

She looked up to see a balding man wearing jeans and a striped polyester shirt standing beside their booth. She laid aside her fork and offered a polite smile. "Yes, I am." She nodded across the table. "This is my friend, Tanisha."

"Don't mind me," Tanisha said. "I'm nobody famous."

"I'm so glad to meet you. In fact, I've been wanting to talk to you about something." He gestured to the booth beside her. "May I sit down? I won't keep you a moment."

"I suppose so." The request caught her off guard. She

hated to be rude to a fan, but couldn't he see she was trying to eat lunch?

"I'm Stan DeWitter." He shook hands with each woman and handed Erica a card. Air Stream Broadcasting was splashed in bright blue ink across the front.

"You're with KMJC," Tanisha said.

"That's right."

"KROK's number-one competition," Erica said.

"A friendly rivalry. I've heard your show," he said.

"The Hawk and Honey show?"

"That's right. You're terrific. I think you'd do great as a solo act."

"Oh, I don't know about that." The idea caught her by surprise. "I think the success of our show is the chemistry between me and Adam."

"Sure, that's great, but I'm telling you, I think you could be just as successful by yourself."

"Are you offering her a job?" Tanisha asked.

He smiled. "I'm saying there's a possibility, if you ever decide you're tired of working at KROK."

Work in radio without Adam? Why would she want to do that? "Thanks, Mr. DeWitter, but I'm happy where I am."

He patted her shoulder. "You keep my card, and you think about it. Call me anytime if you'd like to talk." He stood and nodded to both women, then left.

Erica stared after him. "Can you believe that?"

Tanisha looked amused. "I'd say the man knows talent when he hears it."

She stared at the business card he'd given her. "I wouldn't leave KROK. Why should I? We're number one in our time slot."

"Not even to have a bigger place in the spotlight? A lot of women would jump at the chance. For instance, Bonnie would give almost anything to have a solo slot at a top station."

Not too long ago, she'd have been thrilled at the idea, too. After all, she'd spent most of her adult life jumping from one opportunity to the next without a second thought. But being with Adam had changed that. For the first time in her life she felt…settled. "I'm happy where I am," she said again.

"Carl would have a fit if he heard about this." Tanisha stabbed at her salad.

Her stomach clenched at the thought of what Carl would do if he knew his competition had approached her. "You won't tell him, will you?"

"I won't tell. But hey, keep the card."

"Why?"

"Insurance? After all, if Carl finds out about you and Adam, he could still fire you."

"It's not going to come to that."

"You never know with Carl." She shrugged. "Anyway, consider it a big stroke for your ego."

She looked at the card again. It *was* flattering. And what the heck. If Carl threatened to fire them, maybe she could use this card to convince him of the merits of keeping her—and Adam—on the air.

"Hey, isn't that Stan DeWitter?" Bonnie set aside her turkey wrap and stared at the balding man with the bad comb-over who was making his way across the deli.

"Who's Stan DeWitter?" Not bothering to set down

his burger, Doug looked over his shoulder in the direction she was pointing.

"Program director for KMJC." She scowled as De-Witter, all smiles, stopped at the booth where Erica and Tanisha were sitting. "What's he doing talking to Erica?"

Doug shrugged. "I guess you could go ask him."

"Maybe I should. Maybe I should go over and introduce myself." But she remained seated as DeWitter slid into the booth next to Erica. "Then again…" She held out her hand. "Give me your cell phone."

"Who are you going to call?" he asked, even as he pulled his phone from his hip.

"I'm not going to call anyone. I'm going to take some pictures." She frowned at the phone. "How does this work, anyway?"

He leaned across the table and took the phone from her hand. "Point this. Push this button. Easy."

She jerked the phone away from him. "Okay." She aimed the phone in the direction of the booth where the threesome had their heads together. "Don't they look cozy?"

DeWitter handed over one of his business cards. Bonnie snapped a photo of the exchange. "Perfect."

"What are you going to do with those pictures?" Doug asked.

"Maybe I'll show them to Carl. I bet he'd be really interested in knowing his afternoon 'star' had lunch with Stan DeWitter."

Doug glanced over his shoulder again. "He's not eating anything."

"So?"

"So they aren't having lunch together. They're just talking."

She rolled her eyes. "KMJC is our biggest competitor. If Erica's getting cozy with DeWitter it's like... like sleeping with the enemy."

Doug frowned. "I don't think he's sleeping with her. I don't get that kind of vibe at all."

"I didn't mean literally."

Doug mopped up ketchup with the last of his French fries. "Why do you care, anyway?"

"You don't know how awful it is to be there every afternoon while she and Adam do their so-called sexy act. Erica wouldn't know sexy if it walked in the door wearing a pink boa."

He smiled. "You're sexy, I know that."

Okay, so maybe Doug wasn't so dumb. He always knew what to say to make her feel better. "Exactly. So if sexy is what Carl wants, why doesn't he give me my own show? Instead I'm stuck in weather and traffic hell while her picture is on billboards all over town, next to Adam's."

"You don't still have a thing for him, do you?" Doug put his hand on hers. "I'm not usually the jealous type, but for you I might make an exception."

She jerked her hand away. "No, I do *not* have a 'thing' for Adam. The man didn't appreciate me. He didn't *deserve* me." She turned her attention back to the booth. DeWitter had stood and was apparently saying goodbye. What she wouldn't give to have heard his conversation with Erica. "I'm going to find a way to get rid of Erica, then I'll convince Carl to hire me as her replacement."

Doug scowled. "You mean working with the Hawk?"

"Sure. Why not?" She smiled. "Carl can play it up as the return of the ex-girlfriend. It'll be better than reality TV!"

"I'm not crazy about you working with him again."

"I didn't ask you, did I?" She softened her tone a little. "It's just a gimmick. An angle. That's life in rock radio. You've got to have a gimmick. Sometimes even being a bombshell isn't enough."

"IT'S YOUR FAVORITE time of year, people." Carl addressed the mandatory staff meeting early one August morning. While the new intern, Davie, operated the control booth, everyone else gathered in Carl's office for what Nick referred to as "the annual ass-chewing."

"I thought the big office party wasn't until Christmas," Nick said as he lounged on Carl's sofa, his bum leg propped in front of him. He'd recently graduated from wheelchair to crutches which, he claimed on his show, made it easy to pick up women who felt sorry for him.

Carl ignored the dig and continued. "As you know, September begins the new fiscal year for the station, so we have to close out the old year. That means it's time to take inventory."

Groans greeted this announcement. For one long weekend every August, the station switched to a music-only format while every available person took shifts counting and cataloging the thousands of CDs in the station's collection. Duplicates and out-of-date material were donated to charity or used as prizes in future station giveaways.

It was boring, repetitive work that everyone did their best to get out of. "Ohhh, I feel a relapse coming on."

Nick grabbed at his leg. "I don't think I'll be able to come in, boss."

"Nice try, but it won't work. I'm putting you with Davie, Bonnie will work with Audra. Jerry and Charlie will take a shift, and Erica and Adam can pull the evening shift." He looked up from his list. "Any questions?"

Erica stuck her hand up. "I have one, but it's not about inventory."

Adam gave her a questioning look. "What is it?" Carl asked.

"Your policy about on-air personalities dating each other. How open would you be to changing it?"

Carl's eyes narrowed. "Why do you want to know?"

She looked around the room, confident smile in place. "That new guy, Davie, is kind of cute. I was thinking of asking him out."

"Forget it. There's a reason for that rule. If you don't know what it is, you should ask your partner, Adam."

Adam slid lower in his chair. Erica spoke again, unfazed. "I don't think everyone should be punished just because a couple of people made a mistake."

"Well, I'm the manager here, and I do think so." He set his notebook on the edge of his desk. "Anything else we need to address?"

No one said anything. Carl clapped his hands together. "All right then. Inventory starts Friday."

They rose to leave. Carl put a hand on Adam's shoulder. "You stay a minute. I want to talk to you."

Adam suppressed a groan. Talks with Carl almost never ended on a positive note.

While the others filed out, Bonnie stayed behind. "I need to talk to you," she said to Carl.

"What about?"

She glanced at Adam. "I have some pictures to show you I think you'll find very interesting."

"Did *Playboy* ask you to pose again?" He shook his head. "Believe me, Bonnie, I'm not interested."

Color flooded her cheeks. It took Adam a second to realize Bonnie was actually *blushing*. "These aren't pictures of me," she said.

"I don't have time for this now." Carl put a hand on her shoulder and steered her toward the door. "Maybe later. Right now I'm busy." He pushed her out the door and shut it behind her.

"What was that all about, I wonder?" Adam asked.

"With Bonnie, who knows? She's always bitching about something. Last week it was the fact that she's mentioned last on the Web site. The week before it was her picture on our new billboards." He sank into the chair behind his desk. "The woman is a pain in the ass. If she weren't so popular with listeners, she'd have been out of here a long time ago."

"Maybe she feels like she has to push to get any recognition." Adam never thought he'd defend Bonnie, but Carl did come down hard on her sometimes, and despite her questionable personal behavior, she was good at her job, and popular with listeners.

"I didn't keep you here to talk about Bonnie."

"Then what is it?"

"What's up with Erica? Why is she asking about that dating rule?"

He shrugged. "You heard her. She wants to go out with Davie."

Carl studied him a moment. "That's strange. I would have thought she had the hots for you."

Adam shifted in his chair, somehow managing to keep a straight face. "Why would you think that?"

"The way you two flirt on air—you sound pretty into it sometimes."

"Guess we're both good actors."

"So you have no personal interest in each other?"

"We're friends." True enough, though what he felt for Erica went beyond friendship. "We work well together. We have fun."

Carl picked up a letter from a stack on his desk. "I just got another memo from corporate. One of their stations in Fresno got fined ten thousand dollars because one of their jocks made a lewd remark on air."

"You should be talking to Nick about that, not me."

"I already spoke to Nick. Now I'm speaking to you. You may not like it, but my job is to keep all of you in line."

He stood, afraid if he had to listen to Carl much longer, he'd say something he'd regret. "You don't have to worry about me or Erica," he said. "We flirt on the air, but that's all." *And what we do off the air is none of your business.*

He left the office. Nick was waiting for him, leaning against the wall, propped on his crutches. "Let me guess. You got the-FCC-is-watching-don't-make-a-wrong-move speech." He fell into step beside Adam as he headed down the hall.

"Something like that."

"So, are you and Erica sleeping together?"

He stopped so abruptly Nick almost collided with him. "What makes you think that?"

Nick shrugged. "Hot young chick, unattached young guy. In your position, I'd sure be trying to get in her pants."

"Not every man thinks like you, Nick."

"Sure they do, even if they won't admit it. Hey, I didn't say there's anything wrong if you are sleeping with her. I think Carl's rule is stupid."

"Thanks for weighing in with your opinion." Adam started off down the hall again.

Nick insisted on following. "I heard about what happened at Outback Charlie's."

Adam stiffened, but kept walking. "What happened at Outback Charlie's?"

"Your big revelation that you're an ex-con."

"I'm sure the gossip hounds are having a field day with that one."

"Sometimes things are only a big deal if you make them into that."

He stopped and faced Nick again. "Just what are you getting at?"

"I'm trying to tell you that if you act like your record isn't anything special—that it's just part of who you are, like that chiseled jaw and your knowledge of music trivia—then other people will start to look at it that way, too. But if you treat it like this big, bad secret, they're going to think you were in for something really horrible."

"And you know this how?"

"I know this because despite what you may think, being in this business all these years has made me a student of human nature."

"Is that so? So all the time you're sitting in that control booth making off-color jokes, you're really analyzing your co-workers."

"Not analyzing, but observing. For instance, I know that Bonnie spends so much time trying to get noticed because she's really insecure."

Adam laughed. "Bombshell Bonnie? Insecure? Or is there another Bonnie here I don't know about?"

"Did you know that she has six brothers and sisters, and that they all grew up dirt poor in some shack in East Texas? She probably had to fight for attention from the day she was born."

"How do you know all this?"

Nick shrugged. "I got her drunk one night and I asked her." He grinned. "You should try it some time. A little overindulgence can loosen anyone's tongue, and make them forget their inhibitions."

"Think I'll pass. Is there a point to this conversation?"

"I'm trying to give you some useful advice. Lighten up."

"Thanks. Think I'll put that on a T-shirt."

He started to walk away. "Hey, Adam," Nick added.

"What?"

"If you aren't sleeping with Erica, you ought to give it a try. I could be wrong, but I think she has a thing for you."

"Goodbye, Nick."

Adam headed down the stairs toward the coffee room, wishing he had something stronger than coffee to liven up the morning. Did everyone suspect that he and Erica were an item? If so, how long would it be before he had to start looking for another job? The idea of having to interview again, to face all those questions about his past, made his stomach knot. No matter what

Nick said, people did pay attention when they saw the words "felony conviction" on a résumé. He'd felt them physically recoil from him, seen the sick smiles on their faces as they told him "Thanks, but no thanks."

Erica hadn't acted that way. His shoulders relaxed as he thought of her. She was amazing. The one person he felt he could be himself with.

One more reason he wasn't eager to let the whole world in on their relationship. Right now it was something special and private, something only they shared. And he had to admit, the fact that it was secret, that they had to sneak around, was a bigger turn-on than he'd anticipated. He didn't ever want what happened between them to become ordinary or mundane.

Right now, his relationship with Erica was like no other he'd ever had. He wanted it to stay that way as long as possible, with nothing intruding to spoil it.

14

"DOES TEN CENT Redemption go before the As or with the Ts?" Erica asked as she and Adam sorted through stacks of CDs during their inventory shift Friday evening.

"With the Ts." Adam looked up from a pile of jewel cases. "Why would we have five copies of Pink Floyd's 'The Wall'?"

"Did their publicity people send us a bunch of freebies?" She climbed a rolling ladder and slotted Ten Cent Redemption into the proper place.

"Or maybe somebody…" Adam's voice trailed away, his attention caught by the curve of her backside, showed off to advantage by her short, tight denim skirt. The first time he'd met her, he'd noticed her sexy behind, and now that he knew what it felt like, what it looked like without that denim covering…

He didn't know how long he was lost in fantasy before he realized she'd spoken. "Sorry." He shook his head. "I was distracted there for a minute. What did you say?"

She climbed down from the ladder and started toward him. "I asked if you were staring at my butt."

"Guilty." He held up both hands. "I plead temporary insanity."

"You look perfectly sane to me." She straddled his knee and put her hands on either side of his face.

"Looks can be deceiving." He grasped her waist and kissed the corner of her mouth. "Don't you know you drive me crazy?"

"Mmm." She captured his mouth in a long, satisfying kiss. He loved the fact that she was as eager for his touch as he was to touch her.

"I think I like being with you here, alone, at night," she said when their lips parted.

"We're supposed to be working." But even as he said the words, he reached around and slid his hand under her skirt.

To his disappointment, and surprise, she moved out of his arms and straightened her skirt. "You're right. We'll never get done here if we don't get busy." She turned back to the shelves of CDs, and stopped at the base of the ladder. "It's warmer in here than I thought. I don't really need this sweater." She shrugged out of the sweater, revealing a tight white tank top. She wasn't wearing a bra and her erect nipples were clearly outlined against the thin fabric. "That's better."

She climbed the ladder again and he forced his attention back to sorting the box of miscellaneous CDs. But every few seconds his gaze drifted to her. The station's broadcast was piped into this library room and she was dancing to some lively song as she shelved CDs. As she swayed and gyrated, he thought of how she felt moving under *him*.

He wished he still smoked, so that he could use the excuse of a cigarette break to step out and get some fresh air. Anything to clear his mind of the erotic images she called forth. Not that he didn't fantasize about her off and on in the course of an average workday, but now, alone with her in this dimly lit, secluded room, he found himself thinking about bending her over the stacks and lifting that little skirt of hers—

"I've got to go to the ladies' room. I'll be back in a minute." She sashayed past him, so close her perfume drifted over him, something spicy and exotic. Sexy.

He was standing in front of the shelves, making note of gaps in the station's collection when she returned and slipped up behind him. "Keep these for me," she said, slipping something into his pocket.

"What—?" But she'd already moved to the other side of the room, and climbed the ladder.

He slipped his hand in his pocket and felt warm silk. He pulled out a pink satin thong, with tiny bows in front. He crushed his hand around it, and felt the heat from her body seep into his palm. He looked over at her, but she was shelving CDs, humming to herself, as if she'd given him a memo from Carl or the local pizza place flyer, instead of her underwear.

He moved over to her. She stood on the top rung of the ladder, the hem of the skirt at his eye level. "You're not making it easy for me to keep my mind on my work," he said.

She smiled. "It doesn't exactly take a brain surgeon to alphabetize CDs. I thought you might like something to look forward to."

He slid his hand up her naked thigh, until his fingers brushed her bare buttocks. He squeezed, and felt a corresponding tension in his cock.

"What exactly do I have to look forward to?"

"Oh, I'm sure you can think of something nice."

He slid his hand over to slip between her thighs, his pinky resting against the folds of her sex. "I'd rather hear your ideas on the subject."

Her eyes glazed a little and she took a deep breath and straightened. "Later, when our work here is done, I thought we'd go home. I've got a bottle of Godiva liqueur I've been saving."

"We're going to drink the liqueur?"

"Yes, but not out of a glass. We're going to take turns pouring it on each other's bodies and licking it up."

"Sounds interesting."

"For instance, I'd pour it over your balls and let it run down, then I lick and suck up every…last…drop."

The body part in question tightened at the suggestion of her tongue working him over so thoroughly. "We'd have to be very thorough, wouldn't we? Make sure none of it dripped on to the sheets." He pressed his finger between her folds, feeling the growing wetness there.

"Yes." She widened her stance, and held on to the shelves with one hand.

He was tempted to continue his explorations, but reluctantly withdrew his hand. "I'd take you up on that offer right now, except that it would be just like Carl to stop by and check on us."

"I hope he does come by." She looked down at him, her eyes defiant. "He might get a real eyeful."

He arched one eyebrow. "You have fantasies about performing for Carl? Or is it just the idea of someone watching?"

"The idea of someone watching is kind of a turn-on. But not Carl!" She made a face. "No, I meant that it would be a relief to have everything out in the open."

"You don't think sneaking around adds a little extra…suspense to things?"

"Sometimes. At first it did. But now…now I want everyone to know how I feel about you."

And how do you feel about me? But he wasn't ready for that answer yet.

"Are you really worried about Carl?" she asked. "Are you afraid of what he'll do?"

Not that long ago, he would have automatically denied being fearful or worried about anything. But with Erica he could be more honest. "I like this job, and I don't look forward to searching for another one."

"You have a good reputation in Denver now. I don't think you'd have trouble finding work."

"People always weigh the bad reputation in my past against anything I'm doing now. There are always questions I'd rather not answer."

"You didn't want to answer all my questions, but I'm glad you did."

"I'm glad I did, too." It felt good not having to hide anything from her, not having to pretend things were all right when they weren't.

"We'd better get back to work," he said, and started to turn away.

"Maybe we'd work better if we weren't so distracted," she said.

"Or, maybe we'll work faster since we *are* distracted."

"Still, I don't think it would matter much if we took

a little break." She stepped two rungs down the ladder and put her hands on his shoulders. "We're entitled to breaks. I'm sure I saw it in the contract." She nipped at his ear. "Sex breaks."

"Sex breaks?" He laughed.

"It's in the fine print. Coffee breaks, cigarette breaks and sex breaks." She moved closer, until his mouth was almost against the side of her breast.

"Obviously there are benefits to this job I wasn't aware of." His mouth closed over her nipple, sucking it gently through the cloth.

"Lots…of benefits." She arched against him.

He captured her other nipple and dragged his tongue back and forth across the hard nub, holding her steady with his hands at her waist. She closed her eyes, and was standing with her head thrown back, her fingers gripping the edge of the shelf, totally focused on the moment. There were times, with her, when he could be that way, too—consumed by the present, with no worries about the past or future.

He felt her knees wobble, and he lifted his head. "Are you okay?"

She smiled down on him, eyes dark with passion. "Never been better."

He returned the look, his heart so full of emotion he was afraid to examine it too closely. "So, how long does this sex break last?" he asked, keeping things light.

"As long as we need."

He was beginning to think he could spend the rest of his life getting to know her and her body. A scary thought, so he put it aside, and pulled down on the tank top until her breasts were exposed. "You've made me reckless, do you know that?"

"Good." She threaded her fingers through his hair, cradling his head in her palms. "We all ought to be a little reckless sometimes. You need to cut loose a little."

Her words hit home. Once upon a time he'd been the original wild man. He never missed a party, took every dare, lived every day as though there was no tomorrow. Later, he'd told himself the drugs had made him act that way. But maybe there was a part of himself that needed freedom.

Erica was like a different kind of drug, helping him find that part of himself again. "Maybe you're right," he said. "Maybe I do need to cut loose."

He cupped her breast in his palm, running his thumb along the satiny underside, then up over her nipple. He swirled his tongue around the sensitive peak, then took as much of her as he could into his mouth. He wanted to take all of her inside him—her spirit, her courage, her optimism. All the things he'd lost somewhere years ago.

She was gasping and panting when he moved to her other breast, lavishing the same attention on it. "I don't know how much longer I can stand here," she said. "My legs are jelly."

"A little longer." He urged her up the ladder, and unzipped her skirt and pushed it down.

Grinning, she kicked it out of the way. "Maybe I can stay up here a little longer. You are making it very interesting."

He grasped her hips and pulled her to him. "I won't let you fall. I promise."

Standing here, naked, her pussy so close to his mouth, made her feel vulnerable and exposed, and very, very turned on. His fingers pressed into her buttocks as he covered her clit with his mouth. He trailed his tongue along the folds of her labia, then sucked the sensitive nub, sending waves of arousal shuddering through her. She grasped his hair with one hand, and held onto the shelves with the other.

He continued his assault on her, alternately licking and sucking. Her legs began to shake, and she panted with the effort of staying upright. The tension in her muscles only added to her arousal. She felt stretched tight, on the verge of shattering. The bass rhythm of the music playing in the background vibrated through her, matching the pounding of her heart and the throbbing between her legs.

She came hard, bucking against him, letting him hold her steady while she closed her eyes and reveled in the sensation. She smiled at the warmth spreading through her. This was what joy felt like, she was sure.

When she opened her eyes, he was looking up at her, an expression of such awe and devotion in his eyes that she blinked back sudden tears. "You're amazing," he said, as he helped her down the ladder, to the floor.

"You're pretty amazing yourself," she said, reaching for his belt buckle.

He kicked off his shoes and stripped out of his clothes in a matter of seconds. "I want you right now," he said, grabbing her by the waist and pulling her to him again.

His kiss was hungry, and she could feel his cock pressing hard against her stomach. When they broke apart again, she looked around the room. "The floor's not even carpeted in here. Maybe we should go to another room. Carl's office has a couch…"

"Carl's office is locked. We don't need to get on the floor." He led her over to the shelves again and turned her to face them. "Put your hands here." He curled her fingers around the edge of a shelf. "Now lean over." He reached down to stroke her pussy.

She gasped at the sensation of his fingers on her hypersensitive flesh. "How does that feel?" he asked.

"Oh, yes, that feels wonderful."

"Are you sure?" He slid one finger into her, plunging deep. "I want it to feel good for you. I could try to pick the lock on Carl's office…."

"No!" She shook her head. "Don't stop." Her eyes met his, pleading. "I want you in me. Please."

He stepped away, and she heard the sound of tearing foil, then he was behind her again, grasping her hips as he plunged into her. His hands covered her breasts, cradling her. It felt so good to be filled with him, surrounded by him, adored by him.

Bent over this way, he could move deeper within her, exciting parts that had remained untouched before. She began to pant, feeling her climax building, faster and steeper this time.

He increased his pace, thrusting and withdrawing, each stroke both satisfying and building the ache within her. "You're so beautiful," he murmured, moving one hand to her clit. "I love that you don't hold anything back from me."

She couldn't answer, rendered incoherent by the movement of his cock in her and his hand on her. She shut her eyes and let her climax overtake her. He held her more tightly, and the muscles of his thighs contracted against her as he came with a hard thrust that sent her hands sliding forward, CDs in their jewel cases cascading onto the floor around them.

He pulled out of her, then turned her to face him, and gathered her into his arms. She pressed her face against his sweat-dampened chest and breathed in deeply of the sex-and-male scent of him. A smell that was at the same time erotic and deeply comforting. He held her tightly, and she thought about how strong he was physically, yet how vulnerable his emotions were, at least around her.

Her own emotions had felt pretty vulnerable lately around him, too. She cared for him so much, she sometimes forgot about everything else in her life. She started to laugh.

"What's so funny?" he asked.

She drew back to look up at him. "Carl—or anyone else could have come walking in the past few minutes and I wouldn't have cared. I probably wouldn't have even noticed, I was so into it."

"I'm into you." He smoothed her hair back from the side of her face.

"You were *in* me." She gave an exaggerated bump and grind to emphasize the words.

"You know what I mean." He kissed her, a single gentle brush of his lips against hers. "I love you."

The words were spoken in a whisper, and she wasn't sure at first whether she'd really heard them, or dreamed them. But his eyes when he looked at her were filled with such tenderness, she felt a tightness at the back of her throat.

"I love you, too, Adam. So much."

They held each other for a long time after that, not speaking. Then the air conditioner came on and she shivered. By silent agreement, they broke apart and dressed, then knelt to pick up the scattered CDs.

"It's almost eleven," she said, straightening.

"We didn't get much work done," he said, surveying the box of CDs that were yet to be sorted, the paperwork that hadn't been completed.

She shrugged. "It'll get done, eventually. We can come in tomorrow and help Nick and Davie, if you like."

He nodded. "We'll do that, then. I can drop you off at your place. Unless you want to come back to mine?"

"I was thinking you could stay at my place."

He smiled. "I could be persuaded."

"Good. I've got a bottle of Godiva I just know needs drinking."

BONNIE PUNCHED in her security code on the door monitor at the KROK studios and waited for the click that told her the door had opened. She glanced around the darkened parking lot and shifted nervously from foot to foot. She never liked coming up here alone at night, but Doug had to work and she couldn't put off taping these commercials any longer. She was supposed to have done them earlier in the week, but Carl's refusal to look at her photos of Erica and Stan DeWitter, and his refusal to even listen to her had upset her so much she'd been in no mood to sound perky on tape.

The door opened and she let herself in. She started across the lobby, then paused and slipped off her high heels. No sense risking someone finding out she was here. Adam and Erica were around somewhere, doing their shift at inventory. She was in no mood to run into them and have to explain that she was behind on her work. She'd tape these two commercials for Mighty Mike's Used Cars then be out of there and no one would ever know.

She bypassed the main studio and headed to a smaller one used for taping promo spots like this one. It was across the hall from the CD library, but with the door closed she doubted anyone would be able to hear her.

Once in the studio, she set up the recording equipment, and pulled out the spiel from the ad agency. "Talk sexy," the ad rep had said. "They don't want the usual ad where the spokesperson shouts like all the listeners are a bunch of morons."

"I can do sexy," she'd assured the man. After all, sexy was what she was all about.

She leaned close to the mic. "Hello there," she purred. "This is Bombshell Bonnie to tell you about an *explosive* deal going on right now at Mighty Mike's Used Cars and Trucks. Don't go anywhere else when it's time to buy your dream ride. Mighty Mike has the perfect car or truck for you. No credit is no problem at Mighty Mike's. If you've got a job, he can get you in a car. Mighty Mike's, where car buying is a real *blast!*"

She slipped on a pair of headphones and played back the tape, decided it sounded good, and recorded a second, similar announcement. She uploaded both files to the computer. On Monday, when the play list called for a Mighty Mike's commercial, all the jock on duty had to do was punch it up on the computer and everything was good to go.

She switched off the recording equipment and checked her watch. Time to meet Doug for a drink when he finished up his shift as a stocker at the computer warehouse. And then home for a little fun. She had a new outfit she'd been wanting to try out on him....

A noise caught her attention as she stepped into the hall. A woman's soft...moaning...rose above the music that pulsed through the speakers.

The sound came again. Low and intense, it sent a prickle of awareness through her. This wasn't a noise made by someone who was afraid or injured. No, this was a moan definitely associated with passion. She looked across the hallway. Was the noise coming from the library?

She scooted across the hall and pressed her ear to the door. She heard a man's low rumbled voice. Adam. A woman's breathy reply. Probably Erica. Unless he'd managed to sneak some other woman up here.

Slowly, with infinite care, Bonnie turned the knob and opened the door a scant inch. With one eye pressed to the gap, she could see across the room, to where Erica stood on a ladder in front of the CD shelves. The female half of the Hawk and Honey Show was stark naked, her body pale in the overhead light, small, perfect breasts standing at attention, her face, contorted by ecstasy, thrown back. Standing below her, his dark head bent to the task, Adam was going down on her with intense enthusiasm.

Bonnie caught her breath at the sheer...eroticism of the moment. A ladder! Why hadn't she thought of that?

She stood up straighter and forced her attention away from fantasy. Erica and Adam obviously weren't the mere "friends" they'd led everyone to believe. Now Erica's question at the meeting, about Carl's no dating rule, made perfect sense.

Bonnie couldn't keep a satisfied smile from her lips. Carl may have refused to look at her pictures of Erica and Stan DeWitter, but there was no way he'd be able to ignore this. Adam and Erica going at it like porn stars on station property—when they were supposed to be working.

Bonnie's glee faded somewhat as she realized Carl would never believe her story if she didn't have proof. Damn! Why hadn't she kept Doug's camera phone with her? She'd returned it to him when he'd told her he needed it at work.

She looked around for something—anything—she could use as evidence against the two lovers. Her gaze fell on the studio door as Erica's cries rose in volume. A jolt as satisfying as a climax hit Bonnie as she realized the solution to her problem. She'd record the love-making and give Carl a real earful.

No longer worried about being discovered—Adam and Erica were obviously too far gone to care—she unlocked the studio door and retrieved the microphone from its stand. She hit record and dragged the mic across the hall.

She held the mic just inside the open doorway. Things were really heating up now. Erica's cries increased in tempo and pitch. She certainly wasn't shy about expressing her feelings. Bonnie shifted from foot to foot. She'd done a lot of kinky things in her time, but this was her first foray into voyeurism. She couldn't believe how hot and bothered it was making her.

She heard Erica climb down off the ladder, and strained her ears, trying to catch some discussion between the two. But Adam's voice was too low-pitched for her to make out his words.

She risked a glance in the door again and watched him position Erica up against the bookcase. She caught her breath as he entered Erica from behind, and Bonnie felt her own vagina contract with desire.

Why should they be the ones having all the fun? Still holding the mic, she leaned against the wall just outside the door and slid one hand into her pants to finger herself. Yes, that was it. She closed her eyes and smiled. Might as well make this soundtrack stereo.

And when she was done, all she'd have to do was upload this baby to the computer. Erica and Adam would be history.

15

"GUS FROM ENGLEWOOD had the correct answer to the trivia question. He wins tickets to tomorrow night's sold out Lyle Lovett show at Red Rocks."

Erica smiled at Adam as they began the final hour of the Monday edition of the Hawk and Honey show. She'd certainly gotten her share of good loving this past weekend. Of all the things she and Adam had experienced together, his admission that he loved her had turned out to be the biggest aphrodisiac of all. After they'd finished up at the station Friday night, they'd spent practically the whole weekend in bed.

He returned her grin. "We'll be back with more music after these messages."

He flipped a switch and Bonnie's voice filled the room: "This is Bombshell Bonnie to tell you about an *explosive* deal going on right now...."

Adam muted the sound and rolled his stool over to Erica. "Have I mentioned how hard it's been for me to keep my hands off you during the show?" he whispered.

"I'm having a hard time keeping away from you, too." She reached out and rubbed his thigh, figuring no one outside the room would be able to see them. "I'm not sure we can keep this a secret from Carl much longer, though."

He sighed. "Yeah. We should probably try to arrange a meeting with him soon. Try to catch him in a good mood."

"Is Carl ever in a good mood?"

"Good point. So, is your résumé in good shape?"

"I think you're worrying for nothing. Sure, Carl will probably pitch a fit when he finds out, then he'll calm down and let us keep our jobs. It's not like he's going to pull some bum off the street to fill our airtime slot."

"That's one thing I love about you. You're so damned confident." He leaned toward her and her breath quickened in anticipation. Was he going to risk a kiss?

But before his lips could touch hers, they were interrupted by frantic pounding on the studio door. "Hey, what is it?" Adam jumped up and raced to the door. He jerked it open and Davie collapsed into the room. "What do you think we're doing?" Adam demanded. "We're on air."

Davie looked at them, wild-eyed. "Kill the audio!" he said.

"Kill the audio? What—"

Davie reached past him and punched up the volume, so that the broadcast going out to their listeners filled the studio.

At first, Erica couldn't figure out what she was hearing. It sounded like…moaning. Very passionate moaning.

"How does that feel?" Adam's voice, hoarse with emotion, but still recognizable, asked.

"Oh, yes, that feels wonderful," she heard herself answer breathily.

Adam hit the kill switch. In the silence that followed, Erica couldn't bear to look at anyone. Her face was hot, and she had a hard time swallowing past the knot of fear in her throat. Memories of Adam and her, making love in the library on Friday night, warred with her confusion. Had someone *recorded* them? Who? And why?

The phone began to ring, a shrill summons like nails scraping against a chalkboard. A second ring followed. Then a third. She stared as all five incoming lines lit up.

"I'm outta here." Davie gave her a pitying look, then left.

Erica turned to Adam. "What happened?"

His mouth was set in a grim line. "I don't know. I can't even think about that now."

As if on cue, Carl appeared in the doorway. His face was bright red, and the tendons on his neck stood out like strings around a package. He glared at them for long moments, as if too furious to speak.

The phones continued to ring. Adam picked up the receiver and punched the first line. "KROK, this is the Hawk."

"I don't know what happened, ma'am."

"Yes, ma'am, it's very unfortunate."

"Yes, ma'am. I apologize, ma'am."

"No, ma'am. It won't happen again."

Carl walked over and took the phone from his hand. "My office." He jerked his head toward Erica. "Both of you." Then he turned and strode out of the room.

"I guess we'd better follow him," Erica said, but she couldn't find the strength in her legs to rise. She swallowed and looked at Adam. "What's going to happen now?"

"He won't be able to skin us alive, though he'd probably like to." He stared after the manager, his shoulders slumped. "If we're lucky, it'll blow over pretty quickly. We'll probably be fined. Maybe have to issue some kind of apology."

She moistened her dry lips. "And if we're not lucky?"

He shook his head, but didn't answer.

Maybe she already knew the answer. If they weren't lucky, they'd never work in radio again. Her career would be over before it had really begun.

Adam walked out of the studio as Davie slipped in. "I'm, uh, supposed to take over here," he mumbled, reaching past her for Adam's headset.

She forced herself up out of the chair and straightened her shoulders. Fine. Carl would yell at her. She'd take it, but she wouldn't admit guilt. After all, she hadn't done anything wrong.

Not really. Yes, making out with Adam when they were supposed to be working wasn't good. But she had nothing to do with recording the session, or airing it for the whole city to hear.

When she got to Carl's office, he was leaning against his desk, scowling at Adam, who was seated on the sofa. "Shut the door behind you and sit down," he said, not looking up.

She sat next to Adam. She wanted to reach out and touch him. She wished he would hold her hand, or offer some reassurance that they were in this together. But he wouldn't even look at her.

"I'm giving you one chance to explain what I just heard on your show," Carl said. "What all our listeners heard."

"I had no idea that tape even existed," Adam said. "I cut to a commercial and the new car ad Bonnie did for Mighty Mike's came on. I muted the sound to talk to Erica and the next thing I know Davie's rushing in, telling me to cut the audio."

Carl's stony expression didn't change. "I didn't ask whether you knew what was playing, I asked you what was playing." He turned to Erica. "You care to answer that one?"

She shook her head. Her tongue felt glued to the roof of her mouth.

"No, you don't care to answer, or no, you don't know?"

She swallowed. "I don't care to answer," she croaked.

Carl folded his arms across his chest. "Let me try. To me, it sounded like you and Adam were having sex. Very loud, very explicit sex."

She opened her mouth to object and he cut her off. "Don't try to deny it. I've been in radio thirty years. I know voices."

Beside her, Adam's body was rigid, every muscle tensed. He stared at Carl, eyes dark and angry, but said nothing.

"How long have you two been sleeping together?" Carl asked.

Erica thought about stonewalling, but why bother? After all, they'd intended to tell Carl about their relationship soon, anyway. Though she'd never pictured him finding out this way. "Since the bed-in at Mattress Max's."

Carl's eyebrows rose. "In spite of the security cameras? Who do you think you are, Paris Hilton?"

She flushed. "The electricity went out one night, remember? So the cameras were out, too."

"What about tape recorders? Did the two of you think it would be fun to record your little lovemaking session?"

"We didn't record anything." Adam finally spoke. "Someone else did. And someone else planted that tape in place of one of the commercials so that we'd get caught."

"Excuse me if I find that one a little hard to believe." He walked around the desk and sat in his chair. "First off, who would be listening in on your little private get-together, and who would have the opportunity to plant the recording?"

Erica had been wondering the same thing. She stared at her hands, which were knotted in her lap. "I don't know."

"I don't have to tell you the seriousness of this," Carl said. "You broadcast the sound of the two of you having sex to nine hundred thousand listeners. The switchboard is clogged with calls." His voice rose as he rattled off the consequences of their *accident.* "The FCC will have a field day with this one. Our advertisers will freak. I could lose my job."

What about our jobs? Erica wanted to ask, but she didn't dare.

A knock on the door interrupted. "Who is it?" Carl demanded.

"It's Bonnie. I have to talk to you."

"Not now. I'm busy."

The door opened and Bonnie stepped in. "I think you'll want to hear what I have to say. It's about them." She looked at Erica and Adam.

"What about them?"

Bonnie moved farther into the room. She was dressed almost demurely today, in a pale blue sheath dress and heels. "Friday night, I stopped by the station to record my commercials for Mighty Mike's. I heard Erica and Adam in the library."

Adam stood. "We never saw you."

She smiled. "You were too busy to notice me." She turned back to Carl. "They were both naked, going at it like rabbits."

Carl's face turned the color of a beet. He glared at Adam. "Is that true?"

Adam flushed, but said nothing.

Bonnie took two steps toward Carl's desk and leaned against it, her posture casual, as if she couldn't care less about the conversation or its consequences. "Anyway, I left them to it and finished my work. But I accidentally left my day planner behind, so I turned around and came back for it." She looked at Erica, her eyes glittering with triumph. "That's when I saw Erica in the control room. She was doing something with the computer."

Erica jumped up. "That's ridiculous. I never even went near the computer Friday night."

Adam studied Erica's face. She looked stunned. Angry. All the things he felt. He wanted to believe she was telling the truth. That she had nothing to do with the tape. But he'd been wrong about people before, and it had cost him.

"I was with Adam the whole night," she continued, turning to him. "I couldn't have done what she's saying."

He nodded. Except she had spent some time in the ladies' room before they made love. Could she have set up the recording then? But why would she do something like that?

"She'll do anything for attention," Bonnie said. "Anything she thinks will get her ahead in this business. Look at the way she jumped at the chance to spend three days in bed with Nick. And the way she shamelessly seduced Adam on the air."

As Bonnie herself had done?

"I did not 'jump' at the chance to do the bed-in with Nick," Erica protested. "And I didn't seduce Adam on the air."

Bonnie gave her a pitying look, then turned to Carl once more. "She's already entertaining offers from other stations who've promised to give her her own show. She even had lunch with the manager of KMJC."

"Bonnie, you're crazy," Erica said. She looked at Carl. "It's not true."

"Then how do you explain these pictures?" Bonnie opened her purse and handed Carl a stack of photos.

The manager flipped through the pictures, then looked up at Erica, his face gone gray. "This looks like you having lunch with Stan DeWitter, from KMJC."

Erica flushed. "Tanisha and I were having lunch one day and he approached me. I didn't even know who he was before then."

Pain pinched Adam's chest. What else wasn't she telling them?

"Did you talk to him about a job?" Carl asked.

"He offered me a job, but I turned him down." She turned to Adam. "Adam will vouch for me. I love my job here. Yes, we broke your dating rule, but only because we fell in love."

Was that what they'd done? Fallen in love? An hour ago, he'd have said yes, but Bonnie's revelations had him reeling. Erica had risen very fast in the ranks of radio personalities. Maybe unusually fast. She was ambitious, and he'd been burned by others' ambition before.

"She never said anything to me about KMJC," he said slowly. "I think she would have if she'd been seriously considering a job there." But she'd never told him about the job offer, either.

He turned away from the anguish in her eyes.

"What will happen now?" she asked.

"The FCC will have questions," Carl said. "Corporate will have questions." He stood again. "You're both laid off until further notice. Bonnie, you'll fill the afternoon slot for the time being."

Erica started to protest, but Adam took her arm and pulled her toward the door. They wouldn't gain any ground by arguing with Carl now. Better to leave him to cool off.

As they walked through the station, he could feel others watching them, though no one had the nerve to say anything. It seemed to take forever to reach the front door. He'd had the same sick, lost feeling in his gut the day he'd been arrested, and had to walk past his colleagues wearing handcuffs. There were no handcuffs today, but he had the same sensation of being trapped.

He and Erica didn't speak until they reached the parking lot. "Bonnie's behind this. I know she is." The words erupted from Erica as soon as they reached Adam's car.

He'd wondered the same thing, but Erica seemed so certain. "How do you know that?"

"She said she was here Friday. She heard us. She must have made the recording and substituted it for the commercial. And it got her exactly what she's always wanted. Her own radio show."

"You can't prove it. Anyone could have done that. At least, anyone who had access to the station and knew how to work the equipment."

She stared at him. "You don't think I did it, do you?"

Did he? It seemed impossible, but then, why would *anyone,* even Bonnie, do something like that? "Did you? Maybe you meant it as a joke and it backfired."

"No! I wouldn't be that stupid." Tears brimmed in her eyes. "I can't believe you'd even think that of me."

Now on top of everything else, he felt like a jerk. "You're right. I'm sorry." He turned to his car. "I need to get home."

She put her hand on his arm. "Let me come with you."

"No. I think…I want to be alone for a while. I need to think." He couldn't think clearly with her around.

She released his arm, and he got in the car and drove away. But the image of her standing there, alone, stayed with him.

He hadn't meant to hurt her, but he needed time to try to sort this out. What Bonnie had said seemed to make sense, though he knew she gained the most from making him and Erica look bad. But would Bonnie really do something that nasty?

If only he could get rid of these damned doubts.

ERICA STARED after Adam's car, torn between crying and throwing something. There goes the big, macho man, off to sulk in his cave, while the woman he'd said he *loved* had to tough it out on her own. Didn't he realize she needed him right now? That she wanted his reassurance that they were in this together?

When he'd asked if she'd made the tape, she realized how little faith he had in her. The knowledge hurt, like finding out all the people smiling at you were really laughing behind your back.

She trudged toward her own car, anger growing as she reviewed the events of the past hour in her mind. How convenient that Bonnie had walked into Carl's office at just the right time. And what a coincidence that she knew more about the tape than anyone.

Why am I the only one who sees how suspicious this is? she thought as she started her car and put it in gear. It wasn't as if Bonnie had a saintly reputation. Everybody knew how ambitious she was. She was the type to do anything to get what she wanted.

And she had it all now, didn't she? Her own radio show in prime time, and for once Carl was upset with someone besides her.

When Erica reached home, she stomped into her apartment and headed for the kitchen and started opening cabinets. If ever there was an occasion that called for mass quantities of chocolate and carbs, this was it.

Unfortunately she'd been spending more time at Adam's place than her own lately, and the cupboards were close to bare. She managed to unearth a half a jar of peanut butter and a bottle of chocolate syrup. She frowned at her meager finds, then shrugged. Desperate times called for desperate measures. She opened the peanut butter, popped the top on the chocolate syrup, and added a generous splash of syrup to the jar of peanut butter. Add one big spoon and she was in business.

She was halfway through the jar and starting to feel a little queasy when the phone rang. Heart pounding, she snatched it up. Maybe Adam had called to apologize.

"Hey, girl, I heard what happened." Tanisha's voice was gentle. "You okay?"

"Not great, but I'm hanging in there." She licked the last of the chocolate-peanut butter off the spoon and set it aside. "Did you catch the broadcast?"

"Uh-huh. I was in my car, on the way to the post office. One minute Bonnie's doing her spiel for Mighty Mike's, the next there's a lot of heavy breathing."

She winced. "Yeah. Somebody must have planted that tape there. Adam and I had no idea. I mean, we never would have played something like that on the air."

"There's a rumor going around that it was you and Adam on the tape. Is that true?"

She sighed. "Yeah." Those moments in the library had been so special. She and Adam had been closer right then than ever before. Having their most intimate sharing broadcast before strangers that way, turned into something lewd and wrong, hurt worse even than losing her job.

"Where were you? When?"

"Swear you won't pass this around?" It was bad enough that Carl knew.

"Cross my heart. Tell."

"We were at the station. We were supposed to be doing inventory."

"Couldn't keep your hands off each other, huh?"

"Something like that." Would Adam ever feel that way about her again? If he didn't, what did that say about the professions of love he'd made?

"So how did that tape get made?"

"Bonnie says she was there that night. That she stopped by to record the commercials for Mighty Mike's and that she saw *me* doing something with the computer. In other words, she implied that I must have made the tape and planted it."

"Why would you do that?"

"Exactly what I said, but Bonnie said I did it to get attention. That I'd do anything to make a name for myself."

Tanisha snorted. "She would know about that, wouldn't she?"

"I think she set the whole thing up. That she heard us, taped it and put it in the computer so that we'd get caught. And so far, it's worked out perfectly for her."

"So Carl believed her crazy story?"

"The tape was there. It was obviously us. I don't think Carl cares at this point who put it there. He's worried about his job."

"The FCC already sent someone to investigate. They're going to want to talk to you and Adam, too."

"I know. All I can say is that I didn't have anything to do with the tape being recorded and played on air. It'll be Bonnie's word against mine."

"She's playing the innocent right now. All long-faced about the terrible *tragedy*. But I overheard her tell

Davie the drive-time show is going to be an even bigger hit now that she's in charge."

Erica tightened her grip on the phone. "It's probably a good thing I'm not at the station right now. I'd give her something to wear a long face about. What does Carl say?"

"Nothing. He's been locked in his office. He looks like somebody shot his dog. He really does like you and Adam."

"And we've disappointed him." She felt as if she'd swallowed rocks. Carl wasn't exactly the warm and fuzzy type, but she'd come to respect him. Knowing she'd fallen in his eyes was hard to take. "I know Bonnie was behind all this. I just have to find a way to prove it."

"How?"

"I don't know."

"Even if you prove she set you up, you still broke Carl's no dating rule."

"Yeah, but I'm thinking that looks pretty small compared to this. And even if it doesn't get our jobs back, I'd like to try to salvage our reputations."

"What does Adam say?"

She sighed. "I don't know. He's not talking. In fact, the minute Carl stormed into the studio, it was like a gate closed over his emotions. He even asked me if Bonnie's story was true."

"He just wanted you to verify that it wasn't. It doesn't mean he doesn't believe you."

"Then why doesn't he say that? He wouldn't even let me come back to his place with him."

"Men are like that. Give him time in his cave, he'll come around if he really loves you."

"Yeah." Big if. "I'd better go now. Thanks for calling."

"Hang in there. And let me know if there's anything I can do."

"Thanks."

She hung up the phone and slumped against the sofa. This morning she'd felt as happy as she'd ever been, so in love with Adam she was sure no problems could touch them. Then, at the first hint of trouble he'd pulled away from her. What did that say about the strength of his feelings for her?

She sat up straighter and took a deep breath. She couldn't moon around worrying about what Adam thought of her. If he couldn't come out of his funk and see that she was a strong, together woman who cared about him—a woman who was worth making an effort for—then he wasn't worth having.

The thought induced a flutter of panic. She'd said and thought this kind of thing before—about other men, other jobs. Whenever a situation or relationship got uncomfortable, she'd been the first to bail.

But the idea of "to hell with them, I deserve better" didn't set well now. She *wanted* to stay with this job— and Adam—more than she'd wanted anything before.

She stared at the telephone and thought of calling Adam. Maybe together they could figure out what to do. But the memory of how he'd looked at her as he was leaving the station kept her from picking up the receiver.

The thing to do was to work on clearing her name, then she could try to convince him she was serious about the two of them as a team.

16

ERICA SOON DISCOVERED that it was one thing to have steamy sex with the man you loved, quite another to have the whole city listening in. By the day after the on-air snafu, she couldn't leave the house without running into someone who wanted to ask her about it, or worse, make some lewd comment. She'd started screening all her phone calls, though her voice mailbox soon filled up with people berating her for her lack of morals. Apparently it was okay for rock stars to sing about sex, but heaven forbid anyone actually having it.

Worst of all were the gossip columnists, who telephoned and e-mailed, and even showed up at her door, all wanting "the scoop" on her relationship with Adam.

"You tell me," she wanted to answer, but didn't. The Hawk had been painfully silent since they'd parted company Monday afternoon. Was he still sulking at home? Or had he decided to cut ties with her altogether, perhaps in hopes of getting back into Carl's good graces?

Though she hadn't heard from Carl, his secretary called and set up an appointment for her to tell her side of the story to the FCC investigator. She'd managed to put the interview off until Friday. That gave her less than four days to gather evidence against Bonnie. She'd tossed and turned all night, trying to come up with a plan, and by morning, she had an idea. But she'd need some help. Tanisha agreed to stop by on her way home from work and discuss strategy.

Tanisha showed up a little before six, bearing take-out Chinese, a bottle of white wine and a half gallon of Ben & Jerry's Funky Monkey. "You really are my best friend," Erica said as she unpacked the provisions.

"Nah, I just don't think well on an empty stomach." Tanisha took a couple of plates from the cabinet and began dishing out the food. "Have you come up with a brilliant plan yet?"

"I have. But I'll need you to call Bonnie and disguise your voice."

Tanisha laughed. "This should be fun."

Fortified with Kung Pao chicken and emboldened by most of the bottle of wine, the two friends gathered around the phone. While Tanisha consulted the script Erica had written, Erica wrapped a handkerchief around the phone speaker. "This always works in the movies," she said, handing over the phone. "I hope it's enough that Bonnie can't recognize your voice."

"I'm just a lowly secretary. Bonnie doesn't even know I'm alive." She punched in Bonnie's home number and waited through five rings.

"Hello?" The Bombshell sounded more crabby than sexy this time of day.

"It is very important that I speak to Bombshell Bonnie," Tanisha said in a deeper-than-normal voice.

"What? Who is this?"

"This is a friend. I have some information that is very important to your job."

"What? We must have a bad connection. I can't understand a word you're saying. It sounds all muffled."

Tanisha made a face, then jerked the handkerchief off the phone and tossed aside the written script. "Listen, Bonnie, I know you were behind that sex tape being played on the air during the Hawk and Honey show," she said. "I've got evidence to prove it. If you want to save your ass, you'll meet me tomorrow evening at the Side Street Deli."

"What?" Bonnie screeched like an outraged parrot. "Who is this?"

"That doesn't matter. I've got something you need. So be there tomorrow at eight o'clock. And bring lots of cash." She slammed down the phone and stared at Erica.

"Do you think she bought it?"

Tanisha pressed a hand to her chest. "I don't know, but my heart's racing like a NASCAR driver." She reached for a glass of wine and downed half of it.

Erica patted her shoulder. "You did great." She picked up the phone. "Now for part two of my plan."

"Which is?"

"Adam and Carl need to be at the deli tomorrow night to hear Bonnie's confession."

"Provided she confesses."

"Showing up to meet a blackmailer is as good as a confession, I'd think." She punched in Adam's number, before she lost her nerve.

Light-headed, she waited for him to answer. "Hello?"

At the sound of his voice, her heart leaped up near her tonsils. She hadn't realized how much she'd longed to hear from him. "Adam, this is Erica."

"Oh, hi. How are you doing?" He sounded okay. Not overly warm, but normal.

"I'm okay. Sticking close to home, trying to avoid the paparazzi."

"Yeah. Me, too." Shuffling noises, as if he was shifting the phone from one hand to another. "You heard from the FCC yet?"

"I have an interview with them Friday."

"Me, too. On Thursday."

She'd hoped he would suggest getting together. When he didn't, she swallowed past the knot of fear in her throat. "I need you to do me a favor."

"Sure. What do you need?"

"Can you meet me at the Side Street Deli tomorrow night, about seven-fifteen?"

"I guess. What's up?"

"I can't tell you now, but it's really important that you be there. Just…trust me."

She held her breath, waiting for his answer. Her vision was beginning to blur when he finally said, "Okay. I'll be there."

"Thank you. I'll see you then." She started to add that she loved him, but was too afraid of his response. Better to say nothing, at least for now.

Knowing Adam would be there gave her the courage to call Carl and invite him to the meeting also. At first he was irritated at being contacted at home, but when she kept emphasizing how important it was that he meet her and Adam, he reluctantly agreed.

She hung up the phone and looked at Tanisha. "We're all set."

"Let's hope we've got enough rope to hang Bonnie."

"By the time I get through with her, she's going to be begging for mercy." When it came to the job she loved, and the man she loved, she'd fight dirty if she had to.

"THIS IS BOMBSHELL Bonnie on KROK, your home for the top rock in Denver. Are you ready for another way-out Wednesday afternoon in the Mile High City? If you're on your way home, fasten your seat belt and get ready for a wild ride with the Bombshell."

Adam leaned over and switched off the radio. Call him petty, but he wasn't ready to sit here and listen to someone else do his job. He slumped in his chair and stared at the pale blue jacket draped across the back of the sofa. Erica had left it here Sunday afternoon and he'd never bothered to move it.

Even without physical reminders like the jacket, he couldn't stop thinking about her. How she looked sitting next to him in the KROK studio. The way she laughed. How it felt to have her legs wrapped around him as they made love.

The sick feeling in his gut when Bonnie had suggested Erica had made that tape for her own gain.

His mind refused to believe Erica would do anything to hurt him, but the twist in his gut worried him. Was instinct trying to warn him of the dangers of putting too much trust in anyone?

The ringing doorbell startled him out of his brooding. He stared at the door, and thought about not answering it. He was getting tired of hanging up on reporters. But what if it was Carl? Or Erica?

He heaved himself off the sofa and strode to the

door. A check at the peephole revealed Nick Cassidy squinting up at him, making an obscene gesture with one hand.

Adam jerked open the door. "Nick! What are you doing here?"

"I came to see if you were fighting off all your groupies. Thought I'd cut in on the action." Nick limped into the living room. He was dressed in black jeans and boots, a black shirt and carried an ebony cane with a silver tip.

"What groupies?" As much as Nick annoyed him at times, Adam was touched he would stop by to see him.

Nick settled on the sofa facing Adam. "Now that you're the talk of the town—the superstud whose prowess was demonstrated on the air waves—I would think you'd have women falling all over you."

Adam sank into a chair. "Cut it out, Nick. It's not funny."

"Life is funny, my friend. Learn that and you'll get through anything."

"Is that why you stopped by—to give me a bunch of corny advice?"

Nick ignored the question. "How is Erica?"

"She's okay, I guess."

"You guess?" Nick studied him a long moment, then looked around the room. "I thought she might be here with you."

"No. We thought it might be a good idea to lay low, with all the reporters and everything." Adam half expected his nose to start growing after telling a whopper like that.

Nick's gaze wandered around the room again. "So are we having fun, yet?"

Adam leaned forward, elbows on his knees. "Right. I just lost my job, got embarrassed in front of the whole city. My ex-girlfriend says my current girlfriend did this on purpose and I'm not sure who to believe. I'm having a regular blast."

"I heard the story Bonnie's spreading around. Seems kind of far-fetched to me."

"The whole thing is far-fetched. I can't believe half the city heard me having sex on the air."

A smile tugged at the corners of Nick's mouth. "Sounded like you were having a good time, to me." He shifted, and rested the cane across his knees. "I may be wrong, but Erica doesn't strike me as the type to want to record her, um, exploits for posterity. Bonnie, however…" He grinned. "Bonnie probably makes home movies. And if I ever found them, I could make a small fortune."

"I've learned you can never tell about people," Adam said. "For instance, who would guess you had a decent bone in your body?"

"I never said I was an angel." His gaze pinned Adam in his chair. "But I've learned a thing or two about relationships in my time. A lot of our business is about creating an illusion."

"So?" Was Nick saying that Bonnie was right—that Erica had pretended to love him for her own gain? Or that Adam wasn't seeing the real issue in this whole mess? Or something else?

"You strike me as a pretty smart guy," Nick said. "You know Erica better than I do. What does your gut say about her?"

His gut said he loved her. But that didn't mean she wouldn't hurt him.

"Look, you got your life back on track after your little vacation in the pen. You can get past this little dust-up, and come out on top again." Nick stood, leaning heavily on the cane this time. "You need to step back from that and think about what's real. Things aren't always what they seem."

Yeah, sometimes they're worse. But Adam didn't say it. He thanked Nick for stopping by and showed him to the door. And then Adam stood with his head pressed against the door frame, wishing he had a crystal ball that would show him the truth, and let him see what really mattered.

He straightened and rubbed the back of his neck, thinking. Maybe instead of accepting Erica's story or Bonnie's story or anyone else's story, he should gather some facts and use them to help him make up his mind.

He hurried to the kitchen and dug the phone book out of the drawer. He'd start calling and asking questions, starting with the security guard on duty the night that tape was made. He wouldn't stop talking to people until he got some answers.

BONNIE TUGGED on a pair of formfitting black leather pants and added a metal-studded belt. Leather halter top, leather jacket and stiletto boots completed the outfit. She studied herself in the full-length mirror on the back of her bedroom door.

"You look hot." Doug came up behind her and put his hands on either side of her waist.

She shrugged him off. "The point is, do I look intimidating?" She looked around the room, hoping to spot some accessory that would add extra oomph to the outfit. "I wish I had a gun," she said.

Doug looked alarmed. "Who are you going to shoot?"

"Nobody. But a gun could keep whoever this blackmailing nutcase is in line."

"Want me to come with you?" Doug rubbed his hands together. "I'll keep your blackmailer in line."

She studied him in the mirror. She'd originally planned to handle this herself. After all, whoever had called her was a woman, and she was certain she could take any other female. But what if her caller brought along backup? "You can come with me," she said, turning to him. "But don't say anything. Just stand there and look menacing."

"You're the boss." He nibbled the side of her neck.

"Don't you forget it," she murmured, even as the feel of his lips and his hand and his tongue made her weak in the knees. Reluctantly she pushed him away. "Come on. We're going to be late. I want to get to the deli early and scope things out."

"THANKS, PAT. I owe you one." Adam tucked the padded envelope into his jacket and waved goodbye to the security guard at the KROK building. He checked his watch. He had just enough time to meet Erica at the deli. He couldn't wait to show her what he'd found.

"Adam! Wait up!"

He turned and saw Carl hurrying toward him. Great. The last thing he'd wanted was to run into Carl. "What are you doing here?" Carl asked when he reached Adam's side.

"I came by to talk to Pat. He had something of mine I needed." That was more or less the truth. He wasn't ready to share the rest yet. Not until he'd spoken to Erica.

Carl nodded. "You doing okay?" he asked.

"I'd rather be working."

"To tell you the truth, I'd rather have you working. I thought Bonnie was a prima donna when I had her on weather and traffic, but now that she has her own show, the demands never stop. 'Carl, I need a more comfortable chair.' 'Carl, we need a new billboard advertising the show.' 'Carl, my name should be bigger on the Web site.'" He pressed his hands to his head, as if trying to block out the memory.

"So let me come back," Adam said. "Erica, too. We'll pay the FCC fine. We'll even apologize if we have to."

Carl shook his head. "It's out of my hands now. Corporate is up in arms and they don't want either of you near a microphone until the FCC has finished its investigation and issued a report."

"And after that?"

He frowned and refused to meet Adam's eyes. "After that, we'll see."

"Right, well, see you around." He turned away.

"I'm headed over to the Side Street Deli. Why don't you come with me?"

Adam stared at Carl. "You're going to the deli?"

"That's what I just said. Actually, Erica invited me. Any idea what that's about?"

Adam shook his head. "She asked me to meet her there, too. At seven-thirty. But she wouldn't say what it was about. She said I had to trust her."

"Same here." Carl clapped Adam on the back. "Guess we'd better get over there and find out what's going on."

"THERE'S BONNIE." Tanisha jabbed her elbow into Erica's ribs and nodded across the parking lot.

"I see her." She rubbed the sore spot on her ribs and watched Bonnie stalk across the parking lot. The two friends were sitting in Tanisha's Mustang, scoping out the deli before they made their move. "She looks like Catwoman in that outfit."

"What does that make Doug? He looks like the Terminator."

Dressed in fatigue pants and a tight black T-shirt, Doug did look ready to do battle. "I think Bonnie brought him along as a bodyguard," Erica said. "Maybe she's afraid of us."

"She ought to be afraid of what we have that could ruin her career."

"Yeah, except we don't have anything." Their plan was to have Tanisha say she'd seen Bonnie make the recording and put it in the computer. "Now that we're here, I'm not sure she's going to be worried about your word against hers."

Tanisha checked her look in the visor mirror and fluffed her hair. "I can plant doubts in people's minds. That should be enough to worry her."

"But will it be enough to get her to admit she did it? Assuming she really did it."

Tanisha gave her a sharp look. "I thought you said you were sure she did it."

"Pretty sure." Erica squirmed. "I mean, who else could have done it?"

Tanisha reached for the door handle. "Come on, let's go."

Once through the deli's front door, they stopped to check things out. Erica spotted Adam and Carl right away, together in a booth near the back. Her heart hammered against her ribs. All of a sudden, this crazy plan seemed too real. What if she failed and made a fool of herself in front of him? The two men were deep in conversation and didn't see her. She grabbed Tanisha and pulled her over until they were half-hidden by a display case filled with bowling and soccer trophies won by teams sponsored by the restaurant. "I don't want Adam and Carl to see us yet," she whispered.

"Gotcha." Tanisha nodded to a table near the kitchen doors. "There's Bonnie and Doug." She looked at Erica. "What do we do now?"

"We have to get everybody together, so Adam and Carl hear Bonnie's confession."

"There's a table near them. If we can get Bonnie to sit there, with her back to Adam and Carl, then they can hear what she says."

"How are we going to do that?"

"I'll go in first. She won't notice me. I'll go tell Adam and Carl that they need to watch and listen and not say anything. Then I'll tell Bonnie that I need to talk to her privately at the table. You come up and join us when everything's in place."

"All right." She stepped farther back into the shadows, hoping Tanisha didn't notice how badly she was shaking. "Go for it."

Tanisha crossed the restaurant, making a wide path

around Bonnie's table and ending up at Carl and Adam's booth. The two men acted surprised to see her. She bent low, talking with them, then headed for Bonnie and Doug.

Bonnie didn't look pleased to see Tanisha. She appeared to be arguing with her, but finally stood and followed her to the table near the booth.

Unfortunately, a young man and woman arrived at the table the same time Tanisha and Bonnie did. Tanisha scowled and said something to them. They looked Bonnie up and down and apparently thought better of arguing.

When both women were settled, Erica took a deep breath and stepped out of the shadows. *Here goes nothing,* she thought.

"What are you doing here?" Bonnie snapped, before Erica was even halfway across the room.

"I came to talk to you." She slipped into the chair across from Bonnie. She didn't waste any time with small talk. "I know you made that recording of me and Adam. And I know you're the one who put it in the computer and set it up to get us in trouble."

Bonnie looked unmoved. She arched one painted-on eyebrow. "And you know this how?"

Erica looked at Tanisha, who shifted in her chair. "I—I saw you," Tanisha said. She nodded. "I was there that night."

Bonnie continued in ice queen mode. "What were you doing there? I didn't see you."

"I didn't want you to see me," Tanisha said. "I was waiting to meet Erica and Adam."

"Why? So you could have a threesome?"

Tanisha's cheeks darkened. "We were going to go out to dinner."

Bonnie looked at Erica. "And you and the Hawk decided to have a little quickie while waiting for your friend? Weren't you worried she'd walk in on you?" She smirked. "Or maybe that was the plan."

Erica dug her fingernails into her palm, determined to hide her frustration, to remain as cool as her opponent. "Not everyone thinks like you do. The point is, we know you did it, and we're prepared to go to Carl and tell him."

Bonnie crossed her arms and sat back. "Getting your little friend to lie for you doesn't amount to proof."

Tanisha and Erica exchanged glances. This is what she'd been afraid of. She should have known Bonnie would be harder to break.

"That may not be proof, but this is."

A brown padded envelope landed on the table between them. Adam stood beside the table, Carl next to him.

Bonnie stared at the envelope as if it was a live scorpion. "What is it?"

"It's a videotape." Adam picked up the envelope and shook out the contents. "The security tape from Friday night."

"Planning to sell your exploits on the Internet?" Bonnie regained some of her composure.

"The library doesn't have a security camera. But the sound booths do."

"Corporate had them installed after your big bust-up," Carl said. "They hoped it would help them defend charges of improper conduct by on-air personalities."

"So Big Brother is watching while we work." She made a face. "How disgusting."

"Not just while we work," Adam said. "All the time. The cameras were on while you recorded me and Erica and loaded the recording into the computer."

Her makeup stood out harshly against her paper-white skin as Bonnie stared at them. "You're lying."

Adam tapped the tape case against his hand and shook his head. "I'm not."

Carl took the case from him. "I'm sure corporate will be interested in seeing this."

Bonnie slumped in her chair. Erica thought she might even faint. Doug rushed to her side. He put his arm around her and glared at them. "What have you done to her?"

"Relax." Carl took command of the situation. "I'm going to go back to the office and take a look at this video. You'll all be hearing from me."

"I want to speak to my lawyer." Bonnie straightened, but Doug's arms stayed around her.

"Good idea," Carl said. "I'll have our lawyers call your lawyer." He turned to leave.

"Carl?" Erica called. "What about the afternoon show? Who's going to do it?"

"I'll move Audra into that slot and put Davie on nights."

"Oh." She'd half hoped he'd say everything was all right now, that she and Adam could return to the air.

"The two of you aren't out of hot water yet," Carl said. "Not making the tape yourselves doesn't negate the fact that there is a tape, and it was played on your show."

"But we didn't know—"

Adam's hand on her shoulder interrupted her. "It's okay," he said. "Let everyone look at the evidence and sort things out. We can wait a little longer."

She realized this was the first time he'd touched her since this all happened. His hand felt good. Warm and comforting. She reached up to lace her fingers with his. "All right," she said. "I'll wait." Patience was a new virtue to her, but she was learning some things were worth waiting for. "We'll wait. Together."

17

THOUGH the confrontation with Bonnie had brought Adam and Erica together again, the renewed closeness she'd envisioned didn't materialize.

Her first clue came when she followed him to his house after they left the deli. She jumped out of her car and threw her arms around him, anticipating setting a new speed record for undressing and jumping into his bed. Instead his kiss was less than sizzling.

She drew her head back and looked into his eyes. "What's wrong?" she asked. "That video proves I had nothing to do with that recording of us. That everything Bonnie said about me was a lie."

"I know that." He patted her shoulder and eased out of her arms. "I apologize. I never should have doubted you."

"Then what's wrong?"

"I *did* doubt you." He took a step back and stuffed his hands in his pockets. "Even when I knew I shouldn't—that you've never given me a reason to—I doubted you."

"We've established that. You said you're sorry, I forgive you. Now why can't we kiss and make up?"

He shook his head. "How can I say I love you, then

doubt you? Maybe I'm not cut out for this serious relationship stuff."

He looked so miserable, she probably should have been sympathetic. Instead her main emotion was one of annoyance. "I can't believe you're doing this," she said.

"Doing what?"

Being an idiot. "Being so hard on yourself." She put her hand on his shoulder. "You made a mistake. So what?"

His eyes met hers, the sadness in them heartbreaking. "I don't want *us* to be a mistake."

His words chilled her. "What are you saying?"

"I'm saying I need some more time to think. That we should cool things off a little."

She took her hand from him and stepped back, somehow keeping her voice steady. "You want me to wait while you make up your mind how you *really* feel about me?"

"Yeah."

He made it sound so reasonable. But there was nothing reasonable about the anger surging through her now. So much for her vows of patience. Why did he have to make this so *difficult?* "You said you loved me. I thought you meant it."

"I did mean it. I *do* love you. But—"

"No buts. No more excuses. First you couldn't pursue our relationship because of our jobs. Then we couldn't tell anyone, because of our jobs. Now you're not sure about us because of some doubts that crossed your mind about this whole sex tape thing. I'm tired of you second-guessing everything. Love doesn't work that way."

He frowned. "Then how does it work, if you're such an expert?"

"I'm not an expert. But I know how I feel, which is more than you can say, apparently. I know that love isn't practical or rational or…or necessarily safe. Love involves risk. It means showing a side of yourself to your lover no one else sees—whether that's in bed or out. It means gambling that the feelings you have now will last and grow stronger. It means taking a chance that the other person will find out some not-so-attractive things about you, and you'll find out unattractive things about them—and either those things will matter, or they won't."

She clenched her fists at her sides, fighting the tears that threatened, forcing words past the knot in her throat. "But first you have to be willing to take those chances. And apparently, you aren't."

He stared at her, as if this onslaught of words had dazed him. "I don't know what to say."

How about *I love you?* Or *You're right?* Or even *Give me another chance?* Instead he only stared at her in silence.

She turned and ran to the car. Tears pouring from her eyes, she jabbed the key into the ignition and shifted into Reverse. She only hoped she didn't run over something as she backed out of his driveway.

When she glanced in the rearview mirror, Adam was still standing there, unmoving. Unmoved. She scrubbed tears from her cheeks and sniffed, fighting the urge to howl with rage and pain. He hadn't tried to stop her from leaving. He hadn't even bothered to say goodbye.

ADAM FELT SICK to his stomach. Any minute now he expected to start shaking. Like the worst withdrawal symptoms he'd ever experienced. How could he have stood there like a dummy and let her leave? Why did his mouth refuse to translate what his heart was saying?

He did love Erica. Why wasn't that enough? Maybe she was right. He was a coward, afraid to risk. But with his record, who could blame him?

A distant ringing distracted him. He realized it was his phone, and went to answer it. Maybe it was Erica, calling from her cell to give him another chance.

"Adam Hawkins?"

"Yes?" He answered cautiously, prepared to hang up if this was another reporter.

"Stan DeWitter. Air Stream Broadcasting. I've been trying to reach you and Erica Gibson all evening."

What did the program manager for KMJC want with him and Erica? "What can I do for you, Mr. DeWitter?"

"I heard about the bust-up over at KROK. Sorry to hear it."

He didn't sound the least bit sorry. "And?"

"And I want to talk to the two of you about coming to work for me."

He blinked. "You're offering us a job?"

"Sure, provided we can work out all the terms." He laughed. "It would be the biggest coup of my career to hire you after KROK was dumb enough to drop you."

Adam took a deep breath. "You do know what happened? The trouble we got into with the FCC?"

"Yeah, and I don't want anything like that happening at my station. But the publicity is great. Everybody in town is talking about you guys."

"Right. We're notorious."

"Notorious is good. It gets people tuning in. So what do you think? Are you interested?"

"Maybe. But there's something about me you should know."

"What's that? Don't tell me you're one of those prima donnas who has to have a certain brand of bottled water in the booth, an ergonomic chair and you won't work on Friday the thirteenth. Or do tell me. We'll work around it."

He almost smiled. Welcome to the wonderful world of radio personalities. "I have a record. A criminal one. I was in prison for three years a while back."

Silence. He could feel DeWitter's shock through the phone line. "What were you in for?"

"Cocaine."

"You're not doing drugs now, are you?"

"No. I've been clean since they arrested me."

"We'll make you take a drug test to prove it."

"I can pass your drug test. Don't worry."

"Then I don't care about your past, as long as it doesn't affect your future."

He hadn't even realized he'd been holding his breath until it rushed out of him. He managed to collect himself enough to talk again. "Then I'd be interested in talking to you."

"Great. Bring Erica, too. Say, tomorrow about one o'clock?"

"I'll have to talk to Erica and get back to you."

He hung up the phone, and stood, staring vacantly

at it, DeWitter's words repeating in his brain like the tune to a particularly annoying song. *I don't care about your past, as long as it doesn't affect your future.*

Adam had thought he was being smart, learning from the mistakes he'd made. Instead he had been letting those mistakes dictate how he lived his life. They'd weighed him down like boulders tied to his ankles, holding him back from moving forward with his life— with his job, and with Erica.

He *did* love her. The realization of how much stole his breath. He sat, one hand to his chest, mind racing. He had to find a way to show her that love, to prove that, for her, he was willing to risk everything.

ERICA TOLD HERSELF if Adam couldn't handle all the highs and lows of being in love than he didn't deserve her. But her anger at him couldn't numb the pain of losing him. What had started as a fun fling had been so much more from practically their first night together. She'd felt a connection with Adam she hadn't known with any other man.

She'd thought he'd felt it, too.

For the past day and a half she'd moped around the house, alternately crying and raving, eating too much chocolate and sleeping. She'd made a lame attempt to work on her résumé. Though she'd proved Bonnie was responsible for the tape being aired, there was no denying that was her and Adam having sex on the tape. That might take a while to live down.

Still, she had talent. Listeners liked her. She'd do her best to convince another station to take a chance on her.

Maybe in another city, where she wouldn't risk running into Adam, or turning on the radio and hearing his voice.

The phone rang and she reluctantly answered it. "Hello?"

"Hey, girl, you need to turn on your radio right now." Tanisha's voice was urgent. "To KROK."

She glanced at the clock. Eight-twenty. The last hour of Nick's show. "Why?"

"Just do it, okay? Please? Now."

"All right." She leaned over and turned on the stereo, the dial already tuned to KROK. Avril Lavigne crooned through the speakers. She picked up the phone again. "It's on. Now will you tell me what's going on?"

But the dial tone sounded in her ear. Tanisha had hung up on her!

"It's Freaky Friday here on KROK with Naughty Nick. The rap this morning is about how you know when you're in love. I'm talking the real deal here, peeps. Those feelings that scare the you-know-what out of Naughty Nick. Right now we have a caller on the line who thinks he knows the answer to my question. W'as up?"

"Hey, Nick. This is the Hawk."

"Hey, Hawk! How's it hangin'? Made any recordings lately?"

"You're so lame, Nick."

"I'm wounded! Wounded I tell you! So, big guy, you here to give us the skinny on true love?"

"I've made a lot of mistakes in my life, but the biggest one was letting my true love, Erica, get away. I hope she's listening now, because I want her and all our listeners, too, to know how special she really is to me."

"That's great, dude. Very moving. But you still haven't answered my question. How do you know this is true love?"

"I guess you know when the thought of living without that person in your life scares you more than promising to be with them forever. Or when the whole city hears a broadcast of you making love, and it doesn't take away from the specialness of what you have together."

Nick was silent for once, letting Adam's words speak for themselves. Erica sank to her knees beside the radio and stared at the lighted dial. *Oh, Adam!*

"I just wanted to say I'm sorry, Erica. You were right—I was scared of all the feelings you stirred up in me. I was afraid of making a mistake, but I know being with you could never be a mistake. You bring out the best in me, always. I love you. And I hope you'll give me a second chance."

"Women all over the city are sighing right now and wiping their eyes." Nick sniffed. "You've got me a little teary-eyed myself, big guy. Good luck to you."

"Thanks."

"Erica, if you're listening, give the man another chance. This song's for the two of you."

"In Your Eyes" began to play. Erica switched off the radio and reached for the phone. Adam's number was still on speed dial. He answered on the second ring. "Hello?"

"I love you, too, you big dummy. Why couldn't you say all those things to me the other night?"

"Give me a break. I'm way out of practice on this expressing my feelings thing." His voice softened. "But I meant every word of what I said just now."

"I know. How soon can you get over here?" She couldn't wait to put her arms around him and show him how much his words had meant to her.

"Look outside."

She stood and went to the window and parted the blinds. Adam's car was parked in her driveway, and he was standing beside it, cell phone to his ear.

Laughing, she tossed the phone aside and ran to him. "You big goof. I love you."

"I love you, too, Erica. I'm not afraid to say it, or to feel it, anymore. I—"

"Hush." She smothered his words with a kiss.

"But I'm not finished." He pulled away slightly and smoothed back her hair, which she'd gone back to wearing down, straight and unadorned.

"Yes, you are." She kissed him again. "There's a time for talk, but there's also a time to let actions speak louder than words." She took his hand and tugged him toward the house. "Let's go inside."

"Yes, ma'am." He followed her to her front door. "I'm still rusty with the words, but the action part I've got down cold."

"Or hot." She shimmied against him and smiled.

He swept her into his arms and shoved open the door with one foot. "Definitely hot. And getting hotter."

"YOU'RE LISTENING to the new, improved Hawk and Honey Show. We're here to make your drive home a little smoother."

Erica finished her introduction and smiled at Adam across the booth, amazed at the way things had worked out. They'd met with Stan DeWitter and he'd made them a generous offer to do the drive-time show at KMJC. It was a terrific opportunity.

But when they'd shown up at Carl's office and tried to hand in their resignations, he'd surprised them both by making a counteroffer. He'd sat them down in his office and lectured them like a father lecturing his wayward children—lots of words about "learning from your mistakes" and "paying your dues," in this case a hefty fine from the FCC.

"I've got a lot invested in both of you," he'd said, scowling and pacing back and forth in front of his desk. "If DeWitter thinks he can waltz in here and snatch you away from me, he's got another think coming." Then Carl had named a salary figure that more than topped DeWitter's offer.

"What about your no-dating policy?" Erica had teased.

"The policy's been changed." He stopped and stabbed a finger at her. "But no more screwups. The cost of my ulcer medication keeps going up. You two are going to put me in the poorhouse."

So here they were, back in their familiar chairs in the production booth, and back in each other's arms when the show was over.

"Coming up later this hour, we'll have our trivia challenge, as well as a look at the upcoming concert schedule." Adam smiled at her across the console. He smiled a lot more these days.

"Also a reminder that this weekend at the Civic Center, we're emceeing 'Re-Entry Sunday,' a benefit and job fair to help ex-convicts start productive lives outside of prison." She read her portion of the promo copy.

"I hope you'll all come out and support this great cause," Adam said. "We've got some fantastic rock memorabilia we'll be auctioning off. And if you're an employer looking for help, we'll have a list of qualified, screened candidates ready to go to work. Who knows, you might be hiring the next Hawk." He punched the button to play a commercial and sat back in his chair. "How'd that sound?"

"Great." She slid her chair over and kissed his cheek. "How does it feel, not keeping so many secrets?"

"It's a different kind of high altogether." He pulled her close. "Or maybe that's just you."

"Let's remember you've got a show to do, folks," Mason's voice chided in their headphones.

Erica laughed and rolled her chair back to her side of the console in time to read the next promo. "For the many fans of Bombshell Bonnie, be sure to tune in Thursday evenings to KDEN, Channel 24. The Bombshell is hosting the new reality show, Denver Idol."

"All I can say is, Simon better watch out or the Bombshell will have *his* job," Adam said.

"Good luck to Bonnie. Now here's Rob Thomas with 'Lonely No More.'" The music started and she found herself humming along. "Do you realize I've been at KROK almost a year this month?" she said, after a glance at the calendar.

"We'll have to celebrate," he said.

"We should. It's a new record for me." No more hopping from job to job or relationship to relationship. She might still change her hairstyle on a whim, but when it came down to the things that mattered, she was into thinking long-term.

"Maybe I'll buy you a bottle of Godiva," Adam said, winking.

"Mmm. Sounds good. And maybe we'll find *something* to do with it."

The heated look in his eyes made her curl up her toes in delight. Oh, yes. There was definitely something to be said for sticking around to know someone in the long-term. After all, the more you knew about someone, the more there was to love.

* * * * *

Look for Cindi Myers's
next Harlequin Blaze book
coming in March 2006!

If you enjoyed what you just read,
then we've got an offer you can't resist!

Take 2 bestselling
love stories FREE!

Plus get a FREE surprise gift!

Clip this page and mail it to Harlequin Reader Service®

IN U.S.A.	**IN CANADA**
3010 Walden Ave.	P.O. Box 609
P.O. Box 1867	Fort Erie, Ontario
Buffalo, N.Y. 14240-1867	L2A 5X3

YES! Please send me 2 free Harlequin® Blaze™ novels and my free surprise gift. After receiving them, if I don't wish to receive anymore, I can return the shipping statement marked cancel. If I don't cancel, I will receive 6 brand-new novels each month, before they're available in stores! In the U.S.A., bill me at the bargain price of $3.99 plus 25¢ shipping and handling per book and applicable sales tax, if any*. In Canada, bill me at the bargain price of $4.47 plus 25¢ shipping and handling per book and applicable taxes**. That's the complete price and a savings of at least 10% off the cover prices—what a great deal! I understand that accepting the 2 free books and gift places me under no obligation ever to buy any books. I can always return a shipment and cancel at any time. Even if I never buy another book from Harlequin, the 2 free books and gift are mine to keep forever.

151 HDN D7ZZ
351 HDN D72D

Name	(PLEASE PRINT)	
Address	Apt.#	
City	State/Prov.	Zip/Postal Code

Not valid to current Harlequin® Blaze™ subscribers.

Want to try two free books from another series?
Call 1-800-873-8635 or visit www.morefreebooks.com.

* Terms and prices subject to change without notice. Sales tax applicable in N.Y.
** Canadian residents will be charged applicable provincial taxes and GST.
All orders subject to approval. Offer limited to one per household.
® and ™ are registered trademarks owned and used by the trademark owner and/or its licensee.

BLZ05   ©2005 Harlequin Enterprises Limited.

A bear ate my ex, and that's okay.

Stacy Kavanaugh is convinced
that her ex's recent disappearance
in the mountains is the worst
thing that can happen to her.
In the next two weeks, she'll
discover how wrong she really is!

Grin and Bear It
Leslie LaFoy

HARLEQUIN®
Next™

Available December 2005
TheNextNovel.com

HN23

MAKE YOUR HOLIDAYS *Sizzle*!

SAVE $1.⁰⁰

WHEN YOU PURCHASE ANY
2 HARLEQUIN BLAZE TITLES

11201

5 65373 00076 2 (8100) 0 11201

With six new titles every month, these red-hot reads
are sure to spice things up this holiday season!

HBCPN1105U

HARLEQUIN®

MAKE YOUR HOLIDAYS *Sizzle*!

SAVE $1.00

WHEN YOU PURCHASE ANY
2 HARLEQUIN BLAZE TITLES

CANADIAN RETAILERS: Harlequin Enterprises Ltd. will pay the face value of this coupon plus 10.25¢ if submitted by customer for this product only. Any other use constitutes fraud. Coupon is nonassignable. Void if taxed, prohibited or restricted by law. Consumer must pay any government taxes. Void if copied. Nielson Clearing House customers submit coupons and proof of sales to Harlequin Enterprises Ltd., P.O. Box 3000, Saint John, N.B. E2L 4L3. Non-NCH retailer—for reimbursement submit coupons and proof of sales directly to Harlequin Enterprises Ltd., Retail Marketing Department, 225 Duncan Mill Rd., Don Mills, Ontario M3B 3K9, Canada.

Coupon valid from October 15, 2005, to December 31, 2005.
Redeemable at participating retail outlets.
Limit one coupon per purchase.

52606771

With six new titles every month, these red-hot reads are sure to spice things up this holiday season!

HBCPN1105C